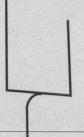

THE QUARTERBACK BARKED THE cadence, and Ty burst from his stance. The cornerback's hands sprang up like dueling mousetraps. Ty feinted one way and dodged back the other. One hand hit his shoulder and spun him slightly off balance, but Ty fell forward and was able to keep his feet. He dug in and churned forward. The effort at speed made his body ache, but the separation between him and the cornerback widened.

From the corner of his eye, Ty sensed the ball being launched far and deep, almost like a punt, almost too far for him to get to. Somehow, he did. As the ball fell, Ty stretched, wide open now. If he wanted even a chance of making it to Super Sunday, he had to make this catch.

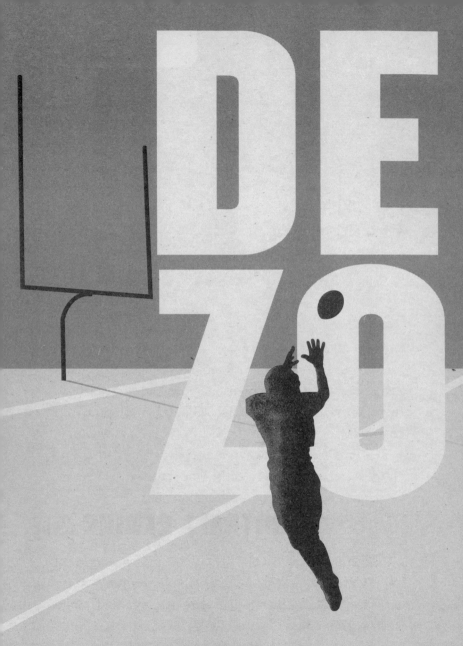

HARPER
An Imprint of HarperCollinsPublishers

EP
NE

Deleted

A **FOOTBALL GENIUS** NOVEL

TIM GREEN

ALSO BY TIM GREEN

FOOTBALL GENIUS NOVELS
Football Genius
Football Hero
Football Champ
The Big Time

BASEBALL GREAT NOVELS
Baseball Great
Rivals
Best of the Best

Deep Zone: A Football Genius Novel
Copyright © 2011 by Tim Green

Library of Congress Cataloging-in-Publication Data
Green, Tim, 1963–
Deep zone : a Football genius novel / by Tim Green. — 1st ed.
    p.   cm.
    Summary: Twelve-year-old football stars Troy White and
Ty Lewis are eager to face each other in a seven-on-seven
tournament being held at the Super Bowl in Miami, unaware that
bad choices made by members of their families will put both boys in
danger.
    ISBN 978-0-06-201245-6
    [1.   Football—Fiction.   2.   Brothers—Fiction.
3. Organized crime—Fiction. 4. Witness protection programs—
Fiction. 5. Miami (Fla.)—Fiction. 6. Atlanta (Ga.)—Fiction.] I.
Title.
PZ7.G826357Dee 2011   2011019391
[Fic]—dc23   CIP
                                                                AC

Typography by Joel Tippie
22   BRR   13
❖
First paperback edition, 2012

*For my boys, the real Thane, Troy, and Ty,
who are even nicer than the characters in this book*

CHAPTER ONE

THE COLD BIT INTO Ty's face. The crowd roared their boos. From the highest point in the stadium, triangular purple and gold pennants snapped like the flags on a castle's ramparts.

"Hey, kid!" someone screamed.

Ty glanced over his shoulder instinctively. A man with a purple construction hat and a stuffed black raven perched on its crown stood at the edge of the railing and shouted until his face went red. "Yeah, you, ball boy! You stink! So do the Jets! Go home!"

The four other men with him wore no shirts, despite the cold. Their bare chests and flabby bellies jiggled beneath purple and black body paint. They hollered their lungs out too, filling the air with puffs of angry smoke. Ty was reminded of the movie *Braveheart,* where half-dressed savage warriors hacked at one another with broadswords. Ty felt like a prisoner, one of the very few people of the seventy thousand packed into the stadium who wore green and white. All else was a roaring sea of purple, black, and gold.

Ty stepped between the benches and the hulking Jets players who sat soaking up the warm air pumped out of the vents beneath their seats. He melted into the safety of still more players, who stood crowding the sideline, their eyes intent on their teammates jogging out to accept the kickoff. Ty searched through the forest of padded legs until he found his brother, tall and lean, built like a greyhound and nearly as fast.

The game would be won or lost in the next few plays, and Ty's brother, the star rookie wide receiver, would likely have a hand in it either way. Thane—or Tiger, as everyone else called him—already had eleven catches and two touchdowns in this nail-biting playoff game. The Baltimore Ravens defense wasn't stupid. They'd be ready for Thane on this final drive, knowing that taking him out of the game would do more than anything else to keep their 27–21 lead.

Ty's older brother looked down, put a hand on Ty's shoulder, and gave him a wink.

"You worried?" Ty asked.

His brother looked across the field at the Ravens bench and the defensive players strapping on their helmets and slapping each others' shoulder pads.

"Just their deep zone," Thane said. "That's all."

"Deep zone?" Ty asked.

"No matter how hard you run, if they're in a deep zone, they're already back there waiting for you." Thane put his own helmet on and snapped up the chin strap. "It's a good way to defend against someone with speed."

"That's you," Ty said.

"You and me both. Fast like Mom." Thane smiled, but Ty frowned. Yes, Ty played the game, too, the same position as his older brother, and he was fast, and their mom had been a sprinter in college. But their mom had died more than a year ago along with their dad in a car crash, and Ty didn't like to talk about his parents. It especially bothered him when Thane talked like they weren't gone.

They were gone. Nothing could change that.

The whistle blew. Players on the kickoff team streaked past. Helmets popped and pads crunched. Players grunted and roared. Another whistle, and the Jets offense—including Thane—ran out onto the field to begin their final drive.

CHAPTER TWO

TY KNEW BEING ON the sideline was a privilege. Only one other boy—a coach's son—got to wipe down the balls and hand them to the officials when the teams switched positions on the field. Ty was special, not that he wanted to be. He would give up his own NFL dreams as well as his brother's already promising career not to be special. But special he was, a boy without parents, and a boy whose only other living relatives (besides his NFL brother) had been hurried away into a government witness protection program. The bizarre and dangerous series of events that had led to that haunted Ty.

Even though Ty still blamed himself for some of the trouble that had occurred when he fed inside information about the Jets to the northern New Jersey mob, Thane insisted the whole thing was their uncle's fault.

It was Uncle Gus who had been the gambler and the person who associated with the bookies and mobsters. It was Uncle Gus who bragged that he could get inside information from his nephews to the violent men who were eager for it.

Even the slightest deviation from an NFL team's official injury report gave gamblers a huge edge when it came to betting. Ty had learned that when people bet on NFL games, they don't just bet on who wins or loses. Instead, the winner has to also beat what's called the spread, the points the team needs to win by for gamblers to cash in on their bets.

Ty had known nothing about any of this when he'd been sent to live with their father's sister, Aunt Virginia; her thirteen-year-old daughter, Charlotte; and Uncle Gus. Uncle Gus hadn't had any use for Ty except as another free employee in his cleaning service. That was until one of his gambling contacts demanded some inside knowledge about the Jets. Uncle Gus knew Thane would tell Ty anything, and he made up a story about a phony website for fantasy football players as the reason for all of Ty's questions about the injury status of the Jets players. When the FBI learned about the scheme, they were hungry for the headlines that would come from busting an NFL player. They cracked down on Thane as well as Uncle Gus. Thane—who was totally innocent—and their uncle—who wasn't so innocent—both quickly agreed to help the FBI put the mobsters behind bars.

Once that happened, the government decided the only way Gus and his family could ever be safe would be to go into hiding. Thane—the FBI claimed—didn't have the same risk as Gus for two reasons: first, because he was a public figure, the mob would hesitate to harm him, and second, because unlike Uncle Gus, Thane had never agreed to go into business with the mob. Only people who joined them and then ratted them out were marked by the mob for murder.

When Uncle Gus, Aunt Virginia, and Charlotte packed up to go, Thane stepped in and said he'd take Ty so that Ty wouldn't have to leave New Jersey and the school where he had begun to make friends as well as a name for himself as a football player. While Ty would miss his cousin Charlotte, a faithful friend, he jumped at the chance to be with his brother, whom he adored with all his heart. So now, living with a twenty-two-year-old NFL rookie as his only relative and guardian, Ty got to do things with the team that other kids would jump through fire for, mainly being on the sideline of all the Jets games and traveling to the away games with the team like he was part of the staff.

Ty tossed a fresh ball to the referee, then slipped between two players to stand at the edge of the coach's box on the sideline. He listened to the play being called and knew that it was a run. The Jets halfback took a toss sweep outside for four yards. The clock kept running down, and the Ravens' crazy fans went wild. They loved it. Each second brought them closer to victory.

Ty wanted to shout at the coaches that they had to pass the ball. He wanted to tell them to throw downfield to Thane. But when the next play was a pass to Thane, it was a simple out pattern that gained just seven yards. Ty looked up at the clock. Only forty-seven seconds remained.

At least the pass got them a first down and stopped the clock, but the Jets had a long way to go, almost seventy yards, for the touchdown they needed. The crowd now seemed to taste a win for its home team, and the cheering became a steady roar like the wind of a hurricane. Jets coaches and players on the sideline had to shout between themselves to be heard, and Ty could no longer get a hint of what play was being sent into the huddle for the offense to run.

Out on the field, the Ravens defenders waved to the crowd, egging them on even more. Ty plugged his ears against the waves of deafening noise. When the Jets offense got to the line, the quarterback had to shout one way and then the other to make any changes. Three plays in a row, the Jets threw the ball. Three plays in a row, the ball fell incomplete. The crowd only got louder.

On fourth down—their last chance—the Jets quarterback dropped back and launched a deep pass. Thane raced underneath it on a post route and leaped up between two defenders to snatch the ball. Thane and his defenders collapsed into a heap. The Jets sideline went wild this time, and the crowd's noise drifted off into the dark gray sky like a dying ghost.

The Jets had a first down now and they were inside the Ravens' territory on the thirty-six-yard line. The clock kept running, though, so the team had to scramble up to the ball. The quarterback took the snap and fired it into the ground, stopping the clock with seventeen seconds left before he jogged to the sideline.

In Ty's heart the dream of going to the Super Bowl reignited, and that reminded him of another dream. This week, he would try out for a seven-on-seven team that had set its sights on the NFL Super Bowl 7-on-7 Tournament. *If* Ty could make that team and they succeeded, and *if* the Jets could make it all the way through the playoffs, then Ty and his brother would both get to play for a championship on Super Bowl Sunday. He and Thane had talked about how great that would be on the train ride down to Baltimore with the team.

"Why not?" Thane had asked.

It was a wild dream, but if the Jets could just make one more big play, the first step in making it come true would be complete.

Ty wormed his way into the coaching box to listen. In all the excitement, no one even noticed him.

"Indiana ninety-eight, Z north," the coach said to the quarterback. "Look for Tiger in the end zone."

"They're playing that deep zone," the quarterback said.

"We know that." The coach scowled. "Get it to Tiger anyway. We got no more time-outs. He got us this far. Take the shot. If we miss the first time, we'll have time for one more play, maybe two."

The quarterback nodded and jogged out onto the field. The crowd started up again, not quite as loud as before since they were still in shock over the big play. But, as the Jets went to the line, the noise continued to grow. Ty poked his head out between two players and watched the Ravens defense. The safeties and cornerbacks began drifting downfield toward their deep zone, putting themselves into position so that Thane's incredible speed couldn't hurt them. Instead of trying to match his speed and run with him down the field, they'd be waiting for him in the end zone.

The center snapped the ball. The quarterback dropped back.

Thane took off, racing past the underneath coverage and heading toward the deep zone. The ball went up. Thane kept running and launched himself into the air at the goal line.

Not one, not two, but three defenders closed on him.

The ball came down. Thane stretched and made the catch with both hands, then got hit by all three Ravens players at once. Thane's body pinwheeled in the air, and he landed somewhere in the pile of arms and legs right at the goal line.

The crowd held its breath.

The players and coaches around Ty stared and gasped and waited for the officials to give the signal.

Someone asked, "Did he catch it?"

Another voice said, "Did he get in?"

They were questions Ty wanted to ask himself.

Then he heard a question that made his heart freeze.

"Is Tiger okay?"

CHAPTER THREE

THE REFEREE BLEW HIS whistle and signaled a catch, but no touchdown.

Then the referee blew a longer whistle, signaling a time-out . . . for injury.

"Thane." Ty started out onto the field, but one of the coaches held him back.

"Let the trainers get him."

Ty watched, helpless, as the trainers and the team doctor ran out onto the field. When the players cleared from the pile, he saw Thane lying flat on his back. His brother's body twisted in pain, and he clutched his knee.

"Thane?" The word slipped from Ty's mouth.

The doctor cradled Thane's knee in his hands, gently moving it one way and another. Thane winced and dug his fingers into the turf, shaking his head. A cart zipped out onto the field. They unloaded a board and helped Thane onto it before lifting it and placing it on the cart. The doctor and trainers walked alongside the cart as it carried Thane toward the locker room.

Ty dropped his towel and took off down the sideline. A security guard tried to grab Ty's arm, but he shook free and kept going, chasing the cart into the tunnel under the stadium and catching up at the locker room. In the back of his mind, Ty heard the referee's whistle, signaling the final play of the game. The Jets had the ball on the one-foot line.

Seconds later Thane's board rested on a table in the training room. Ty stood watching the doctor whisper into Thane's ear as the trainer handed him some pills. The stadium thundered above them with stamping feet and cheers. It sounded like the roof might collapse, and Ty knew it meant the Ravens defense had held. As much as Ty wanted the Jets to win and continue on—all the way to the Super Bowl, he'd hoped—nothing mattered as much as Thane.

Tears streamed down his older brother's face.

"Is he going to be okay?" Ty asked.

Thane popped the pills into his mouth and accepted a small paper cup of water to wash them down. He nodded his head yes.

But the doctor's voice was cold and stiff and it swirled with the growling noise of the crazy mob above. "Hopefully, he will.

"But it's not good."

CHAPTER FOUR

THEY LET TY RIDE in the back of the ambulance.

It went straight up Route 95 from Baltimore to New Jersey, where the team doctor would meet them and perform surgery right away if the knee proved to be as bad as it looked. The lights flashed by outside, dragging their beams across Thane's quiet face like the flicker of a disco light. The wind howled and Ty felt the vehicle sway. The face of the paramedic glowed from the light of his Droid, giving his bushy mustache a hit of green.

The ambulance didn't stop until they pulled up to a hospital in Morristown. Ty climbed out of the back and watched as they eased Thane out and down, rolling him in through the glass doors. Ty shivered, even as the warmth from inside greeted him. They went up an elevator to the fourth floor, where Dr. Pietropaoli, the team doctor, was already waiting for them at the nurses' station.

Dr. Pietropaoli leaned over Thane and spoke in a soft, strong voice.

"I'm going to get you right into X-ray, and then we'll do an MRI. I don't know for sure, but we might have to operate tonight. I'll be honest, the nerve may be involved, and if it is, I need to get the pressure off of it right away."

"The nerve?" Thane raised his head to look down at his knee.

The doctor nodded and touched Thane's shoulder. "If we can get the pressure off soon enough, you might still be able to play. That's our goal here."

Thane's face, already pale, went sheet-white. "Doc, what do you mean, *might* be able to play? I can play, right?"

The doctor pressed his lips together but made no other motion. "Let's just see where we're at. That's the goal, but I can't make any promises."

Ty stepped back and sat down on a chair in the hallway. He felt sick.

CHAPTER FIVE

NO ONE SEEMED TO really notice Ty, and he fell asleep in the heavy reclining chair next to Thane's bed before his brother even returned from surgery. When he woke, sun streamed in through the window, and Thane lay there in the hospital bed above him with tubes sticking out of his arm and nose. The tube from his nose hissed like a small garden snake, and the electronic equipment beside the bed beeped with a steady cadence.

Ty got up to use the private bathroom near the door and when he returned, a nurse hovered over Thane, checking his tubes. The nurse looked like a young grandmother with short dyed-red hair. The deep lines in her face softened when she turned and saw Ty.

"You're awake," she said.

"Is he okay?" Ty asked.

The nurse looked at Thane, whose face looked puffy to Ty. "They operated all night. You'll have to talk with the doctor about the specifics."

Ty didn't like the sound of that.

"Someone needs to call your parents," the nurse said, but not in an unkind way.

Ty's stomach turned and clenched. Even though the crash had happened more than a year ago, the word *parents* still did that to his stomach.

"It's just me and Thane."

The nurse looked back and forth between them.

"Our parents died."

The nurse's face reddened to match her hair. "I'm sorry. There must be someone you can call. You have school, don't you?"

"Yes. I can call Ian, I guess. Do I have to go to school?"

"Your brother is going to spend the better part of today groggy and sleeping. I think if you have school, you should go. Who's Ian?"

When Thane got drafted by the Jets, he bought an enormous slate-roofed mansion in a hilltop neighborhood not too far from the training facility. But the house was a good distance from Halpern, the town where Ty had lived with his aunt and uncle and gone to school. No Halpern school bus came close to where Thane lived. In order for Ty to keep going to his old school, Thane had hired a limo driver to take him back and forth every day, and wherever else he needed to go.

The driver's name was Ian Goodman.

"A friend," Ty said, embarrassed at having a limo and driver to take him around.

"Should you call him?" the nurse asked.

"I'd rather stay with my brother."

The nurse studied Ty. Softly, she asked, "What do you think your brother would want you to do?"

Ty winced. Thane talked constantly about the importance of school and never let Ty miss, even if he didn't feel well.

"Tough it out," Thane would say. "Mom made me go to school unless I had a high fever. It got me into college and when this football thing ends, I've got my degree. You need that, too. School comes first, even before football."

Ty sighed. "He'd want me to go."

"Do you need a phone?"

"I've got my cell phone."

Ty dug into the jacket he had draped over the back of the chair, took out his phone, and called Ian. Ian had a thick Brooklyn accent, and Ty liked the way his voice sounded.

"I got a customer I'm dropping off at Newark Airport right now," Ian said. "I can be over there in say, half an hour. I'll take you to the house so you can change and then to school. How's your brother doing?"

"Okay, I guess. He's still out of it."

The nurse left, and Ty watched Thane for a few

minutes before he clicked on the TV, which hung like a picture on the wall. He went to SportsCenter and listened as they talked about the Jets loss and the possibly career-ending injury suffered by Tiger Lewis on the second to last play of the game. Ty watched the hit in slow motion as they replayed it several times. It was spooky to see the defenders in the deep zone converging on his brother like heat-seeking missiles all hitting the same target.

In slow motion, Ty could see his brother's leg twist in a funny way as he fell.

"Now, this is a knee that Tiger Lewis had trouble with anyway coming out of Syracuse," the announcer said to his partner, "but that was only an issue with the cartilage. This is being reported as a major reconstruction with possible nerve damage."

"And we know what that means," the second announcer said with a dire face. "Maybe the end of a very promising career."

"Well, we'll all be wishing Tiger Lewis the best and a speedy recovery," the first announcer said; then they began to talk about the Ravens' upcoming game against the Colts.

Ty muted the sound and flicked the channel. He had no stomach for sports. The words "we know what that means" rang in his ears.

Ty watched the local news without sound. Images of downtown Newark buildings, police, and firefighters flashed past without making any real impression on Ty's busy mind. It wasn't until he saw a face he recognized that Ty shot up straight in his chair.

The dark, empty eyes seemed to stare out of the TV right at him. The bright red lozenge of a scar in the sunken cheek seemed to dare Ty to look at it, but even though Lucy Catalone's face was nothing more than a picture on a screen, it choked him.

CHAPTER SIX

WHEN TY HAD WORKED for Uncle Gus in his cleaning service, one of their accounts was Lucy's, a sports bar run by the man with the red oval scar. Lucy was more than a bar owner, though. Lucy was a bookie, a man who ran an extensive gambling operation for the D'Amico crime family. Uncle Gus gambled with Lucy and lost big. When Lucy found out Gus was uncle to the Jets' new star wide receiver, he came up with a payment plan.

Uncle Gus could work off his debt by providing the crime organization inside information about the team, information that could make Lucy and the D'Amicos millions. Uncle Gus convinced Ty to help by allowing Ty to play football for Halpern Middle—but only if he got the information from Thane. Ty wanted to play football so badly, he chose to believe Uncle Gus's story about a simple fantasy football website. He told himself there wasn't any real problem in asking Thane questions and passing on the answers. It all seemed perfectly harmless, until the FBI showed up threatening to end Thane's NFL career for his participation in the gambling scheme.

When Lucy found out Thane was cooperating with the FBI, he took off after Thane in a fit of rage and planned to attack him at an autograph-signing event at the mall. Only Ty's quick thinking, speed, and a well-timed shove that sent Lucy tumbling down an escalator saved Thane from a vicious blow by Lucy's infamous crowbar. When Uncle Gus and his family had been shipped away, the FBI talked about a trial that wouldn't take place for several years.

Ty couldn't imagine why Lucy was on the news now, and as he turned up the volume of the set, the image changed to the face of Big Al D'Amico, the boss of the entire criminal organization.

". . . and Big Al D'Amico are being held in federal custody awaiting the outcome of a grand jury this Thursday, when the government hopes to secure additional indictments that some say could put the D'Amico family out of business for good. Authorities are hopeful that years of work will finally put these allegedly dangerous men behind bars, but there is some concern for the safety of the prosecution's star witness, Gus Slatz."

Now Uncle Gus's face filled the screen, and Ty

exhaled a ragged breath.

"Slatz, owner of a Secaucus cleaning service and uncle of Jets standout wide receiver Tiger Lewis, has been placed into witness protection by the government. The last time D'Amico was indicted, back in 1997, the star witness, Bartholomew Higgens, was killed before the trial could take place."

A serious-looking man in a gray suit appeared on-screen. Ty recognized the dark mustache and the tufts of hair bordering his bald head. The writing beneath his face on the screen confirmed that he was FBI Special Agent in Charge Dominic Mueller, the man who had overseen the investigation involving Thane.

"We've taken every precaution to secure the safety of our witness," Mueller said to the camera, "and we have every confidence in the world that neither Mr. Catalone nor Mr. D'Amico will escape justice this time."

The news anchor said she also hoped justice would be served, then turned her attention to the weather.

Ty sat back and looked at his brother's sleeping face. The sickness in his stomach turned into cold, creeping fear.

That's when his phone rang.

CHAPTER SEVEN

"I'M DOWNSTAIRS," IAN SAID. "I made great time."

Ty gathered his wits. He looked from Thane to the TV screen and flicked it off. It almost seemed like the whole thing could have been a dream. Ty kissed his brother's forehead and slipped out of the room. Just outside the lobby, Ian sat waiting in a silver Town Car. Ty climbed into the back. When he first starting riding with Ian, Ty had asked to sit in front, but Ian had said, "I'm a professional. I drive. You go in the back. Don't insult me, okay?"

Ty still couldn't figure out why him sitting up front was an insult, but he went with it.

"Home first?" Ian asked.

"I guess," Ty said, thinking of a shower and some fresh clothes, but also still thinking about Uncle Gus,

Lucy, and Big Al. "Did you hear anything on the radio this morning about my uncle?"

Ian glanced at him in the rearview mirror, his eyes showing concern even through the glint of his glasses. "I did, yes."

"He's coming back to testify? I thought the trial was years away?" Ty sat forward and put his hands on the back of the passenger seat.

"It's for the grand jury," Ian said. "That's how these things go. I'm sure they'll whisk him in and out without a problem."

"It's just creepy seeing those guys on TV and thinking that they're out there trying to kill Uncle Gus."

"That's their business. Your uncle knew that when he started with them." Ian drove down the ramp onto the highway. "Very dangerous people."

"But not for us, right?"

Ian glanced in the mirror again. "You and your brother will be fine. They don't go after civilians."

"Civilians?"

"People who aren't in the business with them," Ian said.

"That's what the FBI said."

"If you're in," Ian explained, "you're a soldier, like in a war. Civilians are the folks out of uniform. They leave them alone."

"But Lucy was going to break Thane's knee with a crowbar," Ty said.

"In a fit of rage sometimes one of them will do

something stupid, but believe me, it's all business with these guys, especially when they've got time to think about it. Doing something to you or your brother would only make things worse on them. With your uncle? They got nothing to lose and everything to gain."

Ty nodded, but felt little comfort in this kind of talk.

"You know what you need?" Ian asked. "A good bagel. While you're getting ready for school, I'll run around the corner and grab you a fresh one with whitefish. You like whitefish, right?"

Ty nodded without telling Ian he wasn't hungry.

"Good."

Ian pulled up the curving driveway and Ty hopped out, going through the side door next to the five-car garage. Ty picked up the paper on his way in and flipped to the back, where a picture of Thane's face grimaced in pain.

JETS GO DOWN, HARD

The headline and the picture sent a fresh wave of dread through Ty. He slogged upstairs, still wondering in the back of his mind if he'd wake up from all this. After a shower, he quickly changed and turned on his computer. The sight of his uncle's face had got Ty to thinking about Charlotte. The last time he saw her was in the back of an FBI car, pulling away and leaving his life, forever. Out of curiosity, Ty had tried his old family's cell phone numbers. Each had been disconnected, as had their email accounts. But there was one thing Ty thought might still connect him to Charlotte.

While Aunt Virginia and Uncle Gus had sometimes been downright mean to Ty, they had been strict with Charlotte as well. One of the many things forbidden to Charlotte was Facebook. Aunt Virginia called it a den of iniquity. Ty looked up *iniquity* and learned it had two meanings. One was immoral behavior, but the second was grossly unfair behavior, and Ty always thought his aunt and uncle were iniquitous to him.

Either way, Charlotte had a Facebook account. She went under the name Fern Arable, the little girl in the story *Charlotte's Web.* Ty always thought it was a clever way to fool Aunt Virginia and he thought that Charlotte might keep using Facebook even though the FBI had forbidden any contact with her former life. Charlotte always seemed to have a knack for doing what grown-ups forbade without their knowing. But when Ty looked at Fern Arable's page, he saw that no new postings had been made since before Charlotte left.

Ty sighed and sent the same message he'd sent to her three times before: "R U out there?"

He shut off his computer, went downstairs, and climbed into the limo. The bagel waited for him in a paper wrapper on the backseat along with a large orange juice. After Ty thanked him, Ian put the car into gear.

Halpern Middle was a good way from home, and by

the time they arrived, Ty had to sign in late.

"I heard about your brother." The school secretary wore a sad face. "I'm sorry."

Other sympathetic faces greeted Ty in his classroom, students and teachers alike. Everyone seemed to know about Thane, but no one mentioned Uncle Gus and the mobsters, and as bad as Thane's injury was, the fear of Lucy and Big Al was what haunted Ty through the day.

After school, Ian waited to take Ty back to the hospital. Ty wanted to ask if Ian had heard any more news about his uncle or the mobsters or the FBI, but he restrained himself, knowing that Ian would likely tell him if he did have any new knowledge. When they pulled up to the hospital, Ian told Ty he had to do a quick airport pickup and take a client into the city.

"I'll be back by seven thirty," Ian said. "I figure you'll want to be here that long anyway, right?"

"Maybe they'll let me stay all night?" Ty said.

"Or maybe Thane can go home," Ian said. "Either way, I'll be back and you can decide."

Ty hopped out and hurried into the hospital, eager to see Thane. He waited impatiently for the elevator and huffed when it stopped on the two earlier floors to let people off. Finally they reached four, and he dashed off and down the hall to Thane's private room in the corner.

What he saw when he went in didn't do anything to make him feel any better.

CHAPTER EIGHT

TY WONDERED TO HIMSELF if discomfort in your mind was worse than discomfort in a blown-out knee. Thane lay in the bed, awake, but staring out the window. Blood had seeped through the white gauze wrapping around his knee. Ty now remembered something he'd heard last night from the doctors. To rebuild Thane's knee, they had screwed down a ligament taken from a dead body they called a cadaver before sewing his skin back together. The whole thing sounded like a monster movie.

Outside the window, snowflakes had begun to dance in the sky.

"They call it Super Sunday, you know," Thane said, his voice groggy.

"What?" Ty wondered if his brother was still loopy from the operation.

"The whole thing. Like a national holiday. The Super Bowl." Thane returned to the conversation they'd had on the train ride to Baltimore two days ago as if no time at all had passed, and Ty worried about his brother having lost his senses. "Down in Miami? The party lasts all week. If your team makes it, I'll go down with you. That's where the finals are, right? Just 'cause my team is out of it doesn't mean I'm all wound up tight. The Players Association has a bunch of events down there they asked me to go to anyway. I got to believe I'll be walking by then."

"I've got to make 'my' team first," Ty said, looking down at hands that seemed to belong to an adult rather than a twelve-year-old boy. Mark Bavaro was one of the former Giants players who lived in New Jersey. Bavaro's son played quarterback, and the former pro was putting together a 7-on-7 team in the twelve-year-old division to compete in the NFL's Super Bowl 7-on-7 Tournament. The team was called the Raptors.

Tryouts for the team—something Ty had forgotten about with everything else going on—were at the Giants' practice bubble tomorrow night.

"With your speed?" Thane smiled until he winced in pain. "And those hands? Let me see those hands. How many catches did you have this season?"

"Sixty-seven." Ty blushed even though it was just the two of them in the room. He held out his hand, and his brother matched it up with his own.

"Look at that. Almost as big as mine," Thane said, removing his hand from Ty's. "You'd be an All-Pro in the NFL with a season like that."

"You want some juice?" Ty asked, reaching for the plastic cup on Thane's tray.

"I want you to be careful." Thane's voice was raspy from the tube they had jammed down his throat during surgery. He took hold of Ty's hand again and squeezed.

"Of what?" Ty tried to sound brave, even though he didn't feel that way. It was hard with his big brother sounding worried. His big brother, the tough, fast, superstar football player.

"I have to stay here another night," Thane said. "They're worried about my temperature. I got a little fever. They said you can't stay here tonight, something about rules and your age. You slept here last night?"

"Where else would I sleep?" Ty asked.

"Well, tonight you need to go home, and I just don't like you being alone in the house is all," Thane said. "After Ian drops you off, I want you to lock everything and put on the alarm and call me."

"What are you talking about?" Ty asked.

Thane nodded toward the TV. "Don't tell me you didn't hear about Uncle Gus. It's all over the news."

"They're in jail, Thane." Ty didn't want his brother to worry, so he pretended he was fine with staying alone, even if he wasn't. "No one is going to *get* me. Does it hurt?"

"A little."

"This is the bad part of playing in the NFL, right?"

"I'll have some juice," Thane said.

Ty reached for the cup and when it slipped, he fumbled with it to keep it from dropping. His foot hit the wheel of the cart holding the tray and sent him tumbling onto the bed and his brother's elevated and bloody knee. Thane jumped and his glassy eyes widened. Plastic bags dangled above the bed; one dribbled saltwater into the vein in Thane's arm. A second bag dripped painkilling medicine. In his hand, Thane held a red button he could push to make the pain medicine drip faster. He pushed it now, several times, and his eyes rolled back in his head before he closed them and lay back.

A new nurse came through the door, young and pretty with blond hair in a ponytail. She gasped and fussed over Thane, frowning at the monitor and making a note on her chart before calling someone to clean up the spill.

"Who are you?" she asked Ty.

"He's my brother."

"Oh, well, I think he's going to be out of it for a while."

"That's okay." Ty sat down in the big chair he'd slept in the night before.

The nurse went about her business, then left them alone. Ty took the TV remote and began flipping through channels. After a while he found an old movie, the kind their mom used to try and get them to watch. Ty didn't like black-and-white films, but he'd seen a few that were all right and this one, *Angels with Dirty Faces*, caught his eye in the beginning because it was a couple of kids running from the police. The ending saddened Ty, even though he supposed he should have been happy that the gangster got his punishment, and he wondered if Lucy Catalone and Big Al D'Amico had started out as good kids who just happened to find themselves on the wrong side of the law. Ty tried to comfort himself that, deep down, the mobsters after his uncle might not be completely rotten.

Thane's dinner came, and he woke up only long enough to take a sip of juice and pump the painkiller button. Ty eyed the bloody bandage, still feeling awful for having bumped into it and wondering if he should tell the doctor when he came in a few minutes later.

The doctor ordered the bandage removed and changed, and Ty turned away when he saw the gory slit along Thane's knee that oozed blood and stitches.

"I don't like it." Dr. Pietropaoli spoke almost to himself before he seemed to notice Ty. "Hey buddy, you can't stay tonight. Sorry. Hospital rules. I know you got away with it last night in all the confusion, but we're worried about an infection."

"I'm okay," Ty said. "I've got a ride. Can I come back tomorrow in the morning?"

"Sure," the doctor said. "Hopefully by then he'll be

out of the woods. Nurse, would you make sure Ty gets to his car?"

Ty wanted to ask about whatever woods his brother was in, but before he could form the question, the nurse led him gently by the arm out of the room and into the hallway. Another doctor rushed past and entered Thane's room. Ty looked at the nurse with alarm.

"He'll be okay," the nurse said. "The best thing is for you to go home and get some rest. I'll go down with you to make sure about your ride. How old are you?"

"No, that's okay, you don't have to," Ty said. "I'm twelve."

"You may be able to tell Dr. Pietropaoli no, but I can't," she said. "I'll watch you go."

When they stepped off the elevator, Ty groaned. Ian owned several limos and when he did an airport job, he sometimes brought out a car Ty called the white whale. Ty hated that because he felt incredibly silly getting into a ridiculously long white stretch limo.

"Do you see your ride?" the nurse asked, walking Ty to the double glass doors. "It's not that silly stretch limo, is it?"

Ty peered out through the foggy glass at the long white limousine, then back at the nurse.

"Yes, that's my ride."

The nurse's eyebrows went up. "That's . . . some ride."

Ty raised his hand in a halfhearted wave. "Good night."

He trudged through the slushy snow and climbed in.

"Hey, Ian," Ty said, his eyes adjusting to the gloomy interior.

The panel between the front seat and the rear of the big limo was closed.

"Ian?" Ty said, shouting to be heard through the panel.

It took only a second for Ty to realize that he wasn't in the back alone.

Halfway down the long bench seat sat a man, a scary-looking stranger Ty had never seen before. He had a bald head and thick, dark eyebrows. When he flashed a grin back at Ty, a gold tooth winked from the corner of his mouth. Fat pink rolls of neck seemed stuffed into the white collar of his shirt. Shoulders and arms bulged like cannonballs beneath a dark overcoat.

Ty knew in his heart that whoever the man was, he'd been sent by the D'Amicos.

CHAPTER NINE

TY YANKED ON THE handle. The door flew open. He reached for the frame of the door to steady himself so he could launch himself out of the car.

Before he could get loose, a hand gripped his collar. Ty's hand caught the molding on the outside edge of the door, and he tried to pull free. His hand slipped, and he felt a sting as the sharp metal edge sliced open his skin.

"Hey, kid, stop." The man raised his voice as he tugged Ty back into his seat. The man pinned him down with thick hands.

Ty's own hand bled. He pressed it tight to his blue jeans. "Who are you?"

The man reached inside his coat and flipped open a wallet. "Take it easy, kid. I'm okay."

Ty squinted in the darkness. Enough light seeped in through the tinted windows so that he could see the man had an FBI badge. Ty had seen one before.

"Agent Sutherland."

"Where's Ian?" Ty asked.

"He went inside with my partner to talk to your brother and look for you." The man nodded his head toward the hospital door. "Don't worry, he made me call my boss *and* some Newark cop he knows to confirm we were the real thing."

As if on cue, Ian's face appeared in the window. Beside him was a blond man in a dark suit. Ian opened the door Ty had tried to escape from. "Ty, we must have passed you in the elevator. Everything okay?"

"The kid got spooked," the agent said. "Tell him I'm the real deal, will you?"

"These guys are real FBI agents, Ty. Believe me, he wouldn't be in my car if he wasn't. Are you okay?"

"I cut my hand."

"Should we go back inside and get it taken care of?" Ian asked.

"No, let's just go home. I'm fine." Ty pressed his hand even tighter against his pants leg.

Ian nodded.

"Ty, this is Agent Chance," Sutherland said.

Chance looked in and gave Ty a salute, but said nothing.

"I'll ride with the kid; you follow," Agent Sutherland said to his partner.

Ian got in up front, and the car began to move.

"You planning on going home to your brother's house and staying by yourself?" the agent asked.

"I was going to lock myself in and put on the alarm," Ty said.

"Aren't you only twelve?"

"People say I act older than my age."

Agent Sutherland shook his head and said, "Well, we need to talk. You shouldn't be staying alone under normal circumstances, and right now things are anything but normal."

"Why?" Ty asked, then his stomach sank. "Is this about Big Al D'Amico?"

"Relax. You'll be fine," the agent said.

Ty felt like he'd be sick. "Then why are you here?"

"Here's the thing: We overheard a conversation earlier today on a wiretap, a couple of D'Amico's people talking about a kid. They didn't say your name or anything like that. Actually, we *think* they were talking about your uncle. They talk in code, but we think when they talk about 'the birthday cake,' they mean your uncle. They're looking for him."

"But they can never find him, right?" Ty said. "If you're in witness protection, no one ever finds you."

Agent Sutherland tapped a finger on his knee. "It's very rare."

"But it happens?"

"Almost never."

"Then why are you here?"

"Just because it's almost impossible doesn't mean they won't try," Agent Sutherland said.

"But why would they bother me?"

"It seems they think that you and Charlotte might somehow be in contact with each other," Sutherland said. "If you were, they could use that to find your Uncle Gus."

Ty swallowed and tried to keep his eyes on the agent. He wondered about Charlotte's Facebook account, if it was possible she'd answered him, and how in the world the mob could know about it.

Ty thought he knew the answer to his next question, but he had to ask it anyway. "And, what if they did find him?"

"Let's not even think about that. The big question is, have you been in contact with your cousin Charlotte?"

CHAPTER TEN

TY LOOKED AT THE agent for a minute, thinking of all the things he could say, like the FBI had no business asking him about his online activity. Something from social studies came to mind about privacy and the Constitution, but Ty knew the real problem was that he shouldn't have tried to contact Charlotte. By doing so, he might have stirred up the hornets' nest of mobsters.

"I, uh, I posted something on Facebook."

"So, you've been in contact?"

"No; not yet, anyway. It's not even under her name. I left a message."

Sutherland winced. "Did she answer you back?"

Ty shook his head. "I don't know."

"On your computer at home?"

"Yes."

Agent Sutherland immediately dialed someone on his cell phone. It sounded like the agent's boss. He said he had Ty, and that they were on their way to Tiger Lewis's house, and he told whoever it was about Facebook.

Ty couldn't hear what the other person was saying, but before he hung up, Sutherland said, "She didn't answer him, yet, but we're about to find out."

After a moment of silence, Sutherland said, "I hope not too, boss."

They rode in silence for a few minutes before Ty asked, "They let you have a gold tooth like that in the FBI?"

Agent Sutherland grinned and tapped the tooth. "You like that? It's a prop. I'm undercover, kid."

The agent knitted his eyebrows into a V as Ian pulled up into the curving driveway of Thane's stone mansion and cut the engine. A dark blue Ford Five Hundred pulled in behind them.

"That's your partner?" Ty asked the agent.

"Yeah," the agent said.

The panel hummed down, and from the front seat, Ian asked, "Ty, you want me to stay with you for a while?"

"No," Ty said. "I'm fine. These guys are the FBI, right?"

"That, you can count on," Ian said. "My friend in the Newark PD confirmed it. Agent Sutherland is going to be driving you around the next few days, but if you need me, you know you can just call."

Ty thanked Ian, got out, and used his key to open the side door by the five-car garage.

"Is your partner coming?" Ty asked.

"No, Ian will drop him off so he can get some sleep. I got the night shift."

Sutherland followed Ty inside, looking around the cavernous space as Ty put on the lights. The kitchen opened up into a living room the size of a small hotel lobby. Ty went to the kitchen sink and found a towel to wipe off some of the dried blood on his hand.

"Where's your computer?" the agent asked. "Hey, is that hand okay?"

"It stopped bleeding. It's not deep, like a paper cut."

"It made a mess of your pants. I feel bad about that. I didn't mean to scare you in the car."

Ty looked down at the stain on the leg of his jeans. "It'll come out in the wash. My computer's upstairs. It's a laptop. I'll go get it."

Ty went upstairs and turned on the computer so that by the time he set it down on the kitchen table, it was booted up.

"You got a wireless network in the house?" the agent asked.

"Yeah."

Sutherland nodded knowingly. "That's an easy way for a hacker to get in."

"But you'd have to be in the house to use it," Ty said.

"Or outside in a van or a car or something. Those things have some range."

Ty glanced out the window toward the front of the house and swallowed. His fingers danced over the keyboard. "Okay, here's the site."

Sutherland peered over Ty's shoulder. What Ty saw made him think he might throw up.

"Is that her?" Sutherland asked. "Fern Arable? She answered you?"

Ty could barely whisper. "Yes."

The agent whipped out his phone and dialed.

"Yeah," the agent said, "it's Sutherland. The girl made contact with him. We got a code red."

CHAPTER ELEVEN

"WHY CODE RED?" TY asked, shifting nervously in his seat.

Sutherland put his phone away. His face was deadly serious. "You're in contact with someone in a government witness protection program. If the mob thinks they can get to your uncle through you, you're in danger, Ty."

Ty saw now that the agent had a briefcase in one hand. Sutherland reached into it and removed a large envelope. He laid it on the table, pulling out a chair for himself and sitting down beside Ty.

"Okay," Agent Sutherland said as he removed a folder from the envelope. "I know you're a little kid, but I got to show you this."

Ty wanted to say he wasn't a little kid, but kept quiet.

Agent Sutherland flipped open the folder. "Take a look."

Ty leaned forward.

CHAPTER TWELVE

ONE PICTURE SHOWED THE face of a young man with a jet-black flattop haircut. He had eyes that bulged like a lizard's, tan skin, and a muscular neck.

"That's Pete Bonito," the agent said. "He's Big Al's nephew, and this is Benjamin Tucci; they call him Bennie the Blade. Sometimes they call him Zipper."

While Bonito looked like a stone-cold killer, Bennie the Blade appeared harmless, scrawny, with pale, blotchy skin, a tuft of reddish orange hair, and eyes that looked wet and irritated.

"Zipper?" Ty said.

"Let's just say he's dangerous."

"You can tell me."

Sutherland sighed. "Okay. He uses a knife when he kills people. Opens their bellies like you unzip your jacket, just *zip zip*."

Ty clutched his stomach. "Why are you showing me these guys?"

Sutherland cleared his throat. "These are the guys we heard on the wiretap. They seem to have filled in for Big Al and Lucy, Bonito for his uncle as acting boss, and the Blade for Lucy running the gambling books. These guys are like roaches. You squash a couple of them, and two more jump right into their spots."

"But they want my uncle, not me."

Sutherland pressed his lips together before he spoke. "You're in touch with your cousin, and we think they may know about it."

Sutherland seemed to study Ty's face. "Maybe we're wrong, but if we're not, they're going to try to get to you before your uncle comes into town. This is going to be their only chance to get at him until the trial. If they could find out the details of his trip, it wouldn't be hard for them to make a plan that would silence him for good. That's why I'm going to keep an eye on you, and I want you to know what these people look like so you can keep an eye out yourself. With your uncle out of the way, the government has no case. Big Al and Lucy would go free tomorrow."

"But you're just guessing they want to talk to me?" Ty asked.

"It's more than a guess." Agent Sutherland grimaced. "The Blade said he'd pay the kid a visit."

"But that could be Bennie the Blade's own kid they were talking about," Ty said, feeling suddenly hopeful.

Then Sutherland shook his head and said, "The Blade doesn't have any kids. In fact, he hates kids."

CHAPTER THIRTEEN

"THEN I'VE GOT TO hide, like Charlotte," Ty said, looking around at the beautiful home he lived in with his brother and fearful at the thought of going into hiding and having to live once again with a grouchy aunt and an obnoxious uncle who drank too much beer.

"They're not going to hurt you," Agent Sutherland said, shaking his head. "They'll just try to scare the information out of you, but I'm not going to let that happen. And once we get past this grand jury testimony, they won't be bothering with you."

"Why won't they?"

"If they think you know something? Trust me, they'll make their move before your uncle testifies to the grand jury. Then they'll see us and they'll know that *we* know."

"I don't see how that makes me safe," Ty said with a moan.

"When they know we're on to them, they'll also know that we're going to move Gus to a new place and cut off any communication between you and your cousin."

"They have to move again?" Ty felt horrible.

Sutherland nodded. "You don't think we can keep them where they are, do you? The whole thing's been compromised. So, once he's been here and gone, you'll be safe. No more Facebook, though, right?"

"No." Ty shook his head. "Thursday. Three days."

"Yeah, well, you better get to sleep, right, kid? You sure that hand is okay?"

Ty looked down at the crusty blood along the thin slice. "I'm fine."

"Okay. I'll be right here. Shout if you need me."

"My brother said to put the alarm on."

"You can do that."

"Just don't open any doors or windows."

"Got it," the agent said, taking some paperwork and a computer out of his briefcase and setting them in front of him on the table.

Ty looked over his shoulder before he left the room. He went upstairs and put on the alarm, punching the code into the keypad in the hallway between his and Thane's bedrooms. After getting ready for bed, Ty dialed his brother's cell phone like Thane had asked, but all he got was voice mail. Ty figured the pain medicine still had Thane out cold, so he left a message and clicked his phone shut. After he turned out the light, Ty peered through the curtains of his bedroom window down at the street, empty except for the FBI car in the driveway. In the army of shadows it wasn't hard for Ty to imagine the Blade and Bonito out there somewhere. He tried to focus on the agent downstairs, sitting alert at the kitchen table.

"Like a big guard dog." Ty spoke out loud, comforting himself with the sound of the words, and he climbed into bed, pulling the covers up over his head.

The wind groaned against the stone house and its slate roof. Ty tried not to hear the Blade's past victims in the moaning wind, but his sleep was fitful. His hand began to throb and his dreams were scary, and in the morning he certainly didn't want to get up for school.

When he woke, Ty reached out from under his covers to turn on the light and felt better once it was on. He climbed out of bed and turned on all the lights, peering out through the curtains at the street below, searching for signs of a big black Cadillac like the one he'd heard Al D'Amico drove before they locked him up. He felt better at the sight of the Ford Five Hundred.

Ty examined his hand. There was no new bleeding, but the skin around the cut was puffy. He winced as he dabbed on some ointment to keep it from getting infected and wrapped it in gauze to protect it. He dialed Thane and got voice mail, the same as before bed. He looked at the clock and hurried to get ready.

Downstairs, Agent Sutherland was right where Ty had left him, bent over his work and clacking away at the computer.

"Still at it?" Ty asked.

"Lots of paperwork," the agent said. "They don't tell you that part. You think it's about guns and manhunts, but a lot of being in law enforcement is just clicking a keyboard."

Ty offered the agent some breakfast, but Sutherland said he didn't like to eat before he slept and that he would be taking a few hours off after he dropped Ty at school. As Ty sat crunching on Cheerios doused with milk, his mind turned to the 7-on-7 tryouts. He flexed his hand and wondered how well he'd be able to catch the ball. He pushed the doubts from his mind, drank down his orange juice, and rinsed his dishes before tucking them into the dishwasher.

That's when his cell phone rang. Ty looked at the number and recognized it as coming from the hospital.

He answered. "Thane?"

"No," said a man with a husky voice. "This isn't Thane. I'm Dr. Suarez. Is this Ty?"

"Yes." Ty swallowed. "Is my brother okay?"

The doctor went silent for a moment before he spoke. "No, Ty. I'm afraid he's not."

CHAPTER FOURTEEN

EVEN THOUGH TY LOVED books and Avi was one of his favorite writers, Ty would never finish Crispin. The main character had only just met an enormous and hairy jester when someone knocked at Ty's front door. Ty put the book he would never read again down on the lamp table. As he crossed the smoky room, he made a mental note to put another log in the wood-burning stove. He wore slippers and a sweater to fend off the cold.

Ty's family lived on a wooded ridge in the country and they didn't get many people knocking at their door. The sight of a tall man outside on the front step wearing a trooper's hat made his heart jump. Ty opened the door, and cold air stormed the entryway. The trooper had eyes as dark as black marbles and eyebrows so thick they seemed made for winter. The eyes were serious and *sad in a way Ty had never seen before.*

"Are you Ty Lewis?"

"Yes." The word barely followed the wisp of steam that escaped his lips.

"Can I come in?"

"Why?"

"I think you should sit down."

"No. Tell me. Tell me, now."

"I'm sorry, son," the trooper said, shifting his feet so that the polished black shoes crunched the bits of ice on the front step. "There's been an accident. Your parents are both dead."

Ty had never felt a weight so heavy before or since, but the doctor's voice on the phone came awfully close and reminded him of that moment only a year before.

"Where is he?" Ty asked the doctor.

"He's here," the doctor said. "He's sleeping now, but he made me promise I'd call you in the morning. It was the only way I could get him to settle down. He's developed an infection. It happens every so often."

"But, he'll be okay?"

"He's fighting it."

"That's not okay," Ty said, the panic rising like a flood, ready to choke him to death. "He'll be okay, right?"

"He's very strong, Ty, but I'm not going to tell you it isn't serious. It is. We moved him to intensive care as a precaution."

Tears spilled down Ty's cheeks and dripped onto the place mat in front of him. He shook his head.

Choking, he asked, "Can I see him?"

"You can't go into ICU, son," the doctor said. "The nurse told me you live with your brother? You have no other relatives?"

Ty felt like he was tumbling in empty space and he choked on the word. "No."

"Well." The doctor paused. "We'll get a caseworker from the county to look in on you if your brother isn't out of ICU by the end of the day. Do you take the bus to school?"

"I have a ride." The word *caseworker* flashed in his mind like the light on a police car. His last caseworker had stuck him with Uncle Gus, who had him cleaning toilets and sleeping on a mattress in the laundry room like a dog.

"Okay, good. You can call me later today, after school. We may know more."

CHAPTER FIFTEEN

"WHAT'S WRONG?" AGENT SUTHERLAND asked as Ty pocketed his phone.

"My brother's not doing well." Ty flexed his aching hand.

"You want to go to the hospital?" the agent asked.

Ty looked away. "The doctor said I should go to school. Thane's got an infection. He's in ICU, intensive care."

"My uncle was in intensive care for a week after open-heart surgery." The agent's voice was lighthearted. "That was like, four years ago. He whipped me in tennis last week. Your brother? They didn't invent an infection that can take him down. Don't worry, kid."

On the ride to school, Agent Sutherland told the full story of his uncle. When they pulled up to the school, the agent got out and looked around like some kind of bodyguard. A second car the same make as Sutherland's pulled up; Ty saw that it was Agent Chance.

"He'll be outside the school while I go and get some sleep," Sutherland said. "I'll be back by three when you come out."

Ty shook hands with the other agent, using his left hand. He liked the warmth in Chance's blue eyes, but still he asked Sutherland, "You think I'm safe?"

"In school? You're fine. And hey, I keep saying it: your brother will be fine, too."

Ty said thanks and headed for the entrance. Behind him, the FBI agents stood like statues, watching.

The kids milling toward the entrance to Halpern Middle didn't even blink at the sight of the two men, even though Sutherland stuck out like a sore thumb with his bald head and gold tooth. Ty's schoolmates were used to a lot of strange things, from NFL players to white limousines. It was part of the legend that Ty Lewis had become, first showing up as an unlucky orphan, a skinny, quiet geek of a kid with small round glasses, toting his books around in a musty pillowcase, and a way of not looking people in the eye. Then his older brother became the Jets' first-round draft pick, and Ty transformed into a star football player himself. He made the news for his role in saving his brother from the crowbar of what people called a "mafia maniac" and also helped Halpern Middle win a county football championship.

Ty couldn't help wishing he was just a normal kid, back in Tully with both his parents. When he got to the top of the school's steps, he looked past the FBI agents, scanning the street and half expecting to see Bonito's leering face go by in a big dark SUV. There was nothing but soccer moms and classmates.

Ty didn't love school, but he didn't mind it. He had a great English teacher named Judy Weisman who never recommended a bad book, and a history teacher, Mr. Salter, who somehow made even the War of 1812 fun. In gym class, Coach V was doing volleyball, and even playing with just one hand was challenging enough to make the day move faster. After the final bell rang, Ty spotted the FBI agent's car outside the school.

As he walked down the concrete steps, he dialed Thane's doctor's number, but only got voice mail. He left a message, and got into the front seat.

"Can we go to the hospital?" Ty asked.

"Agent Chance stopped by there a half hour ago, kid," Sutherland said. "Your brother is still in the tank. That's what I called it with my uncle, 'cause it's kind of like a fish tank; you know, all the tubes and little blinking lights, and you can only watch through the glass."

"I want to see him."

"Well, we can try, right?" Agent Sutherland put the government car into gear, and they took off for the hospital.

"It's weird." Ty huffed his breath on the window.

"It's like, they can't be out there, looking to grab me or something. Then I remember Lucy looking at me the way he did and the sound of him slapping that crowbar he always used to carry against his hand, and I know that they *are* out there."

"They're out there," Sutherland said, "but we don't know for certain they're going to try to get you. We're just playing it safe, Ty."

"I know. Believe me, if my brother's okay, I'll be happy to run from the mob for the rest of my life."

"We're not running," Agent Sutherland said. "I told you, we're just playing it safe."

Ty nodded but stayed quiet for the rest of the ride. When Sutherland let him out, Ty noticed how the agent scanned the area around them and kept looking over his shoulder as he walked Ty into the hospital.

Thane was on a different floor, and they wouldn't let Ty in. Dr. Suarez was a short man with small green eyes and black hair. The front pocket of his white coat sagged with a handful of pens and a light for looking into people's ears. He met Ty and the agent in a small waiting room by the nurses' station.

"Who are you?" the doctor asked Sutherland.

Sutherland smoothed the sleeves of his suit coat and explained, and the doctor acted like everyone who came in had an FBI bodyguard.

"I've got a county caseworker lined up to take care of the boy," the doctor said.

"We can handle it for a day or so," Agent Sutherland said, winking at Ty.

The doctor nodded and turned to Ty. "Your brother's a little better, but not out of the woods."

"Can I see him?" Ty asked.

"Not yet. He wanted me to give you a message though." The doctor removed a pad from his side pocket and flipped through it. "He was pretty upset and he said to tell you to make sure you 'go to seven'? I'm not sure what that means. Then he said something about 'Super Sunday.' Does any of that make sense to you?"

"Yes. I know what he wants."

"Okay. I'm sorry about not seeing him. That's just the rules with ICU."

"Can't we just look?" Agent Sutherland said. "When my uncle was in the ICU, we could at least stand in the hallway and wave at him through the glass. I was telling Ty, it was like a fish tank."

The doctor scowled at the FBI agent. "We don't do that here."

The agent shrugged.

"Hopefully tomorrow," the doctor said to Ty before turning and walking away.

CHAPTER SIXTEEN

"SO, WHAT'S THIS SEVEN thing, if you don't mind my asking?" Agent Sutherland wheeled the car out of the hospital parking lot, checking the rearview mirror, presumably for mobsters.

"Seven-on-Seven." Ty explained the team Mark Bavaro was putting together. "Tryouts are at five thirty tonight at the Giants' practice facility. My brother got me in, but with my hand? I don't know if it's even worth it."

"Cut's deeper than you thought, huh?"

"Deep enough."

"Well," the agent said, "football's a tough game."

"I'm tough."

"I can see that in your eyes."

Ty smiled. "Can we get something to eat before the tryouts?"

"Uncle Sam won't spring for much more than a cheeseburger."

"I love cheeseburgers."

They stopped at a roadside stand Agent Sutherland said he'd been going to for twenty years. The people behind the counter wore red-and-white-striped paper caps, and the patrons sat huddled around the small tables without removing their coats.

Ty wiped some grease from his mouth and asked, "How old are you?"

"Why? I look old?"

"To me."

"Thirty-two. Old?"

"Yeah."

"You think you're gonna make this team?" Agent Sutherland stabbed a fry into his mouth. "I remember watching Bavaro when I was a kid. The Giants won the Super Bowl. My dad painted his face blue."

"I'm fast, like my brother." Ty flexed his hand, wincing. "I've got good hands, too, but this isn't good."

"You keep going back to that."

"If I don't make it."

"I bet your brother doesn't make excuses."

Ty put his hand down. "What's that supposed to mean?"

"Those NFL guys? They're out of their minds with determination. No excuses for them. Excuses give you an escape hatch. You can always quit at the end and get away from the real pain because you got that excuse."

Sutherland wadded up the paper wrappings and jammed them into his empty soda cup. "Thing is, you never really do the best you can do. You gotta go into it without excuses. Sometimes you fail. Life's like that."

"Were you a football player?"

"Me? No. Wrestler. East Stroudsburg. Second in the NCAA, Division Two."

"Second?"

"I had a bad Achilles."

"An excuse?"

Sutherland stood up and checked his watch. "You don't want to be late for Mark Bavaro. That guy is old-school."

"You know him?" Ty asked as they got into the car.

"I told you, I saw him play." Sutherland pulled out onto the road. "How's his son?"

"Great. He's twelve and everyone says he can really throw. My brother made some calls to get me a tryout. My team won the county championship and I was the MVP."

"Following in your brother's footsteps, huh?"

Ty looked out the window at the passing utility poles. Dead cattails waved from the frozen swamps. Ice bearded the dark and rusted bridges spanning the waterways. The darkening sky held no birds, only blinking airplanes headed for Newark. "I'd like to."

"And you don't mind just going alone, showing up with an FBI agent?"

"No."

"Lots of kids wouldn't feel comfortable with that."

"I've been alone before." Ty turned his attention to the agent. "As long as I know I've got my brother out there, I don't even think of it like being alone."

"I see."

The Giants' indoor practice facility looked like a big white barn next to the team offices. In the distance stood the new stadium. A security guard checked Ty's name at the door, and Agent Sutherland got around any explanations with his FBI identification.

Inside, Ty felt like Pinocchio in the belly of the whale. Enormous arches of steel ran like the whale's ribs for eighty yards, and the boys already there darted about on the green plastic grass like krill. The vast space swallowed up shouts and commands without offering up an echo. Ty flexed his damaged hand, and a shiver scampered down his backbone.

Mark Bavaro stood at the center of it all, wearing a Giants cap and a heavy gray sweatshirt and pants. Ty laced his cleats up tight and jogged out to the middle with the rest of them when Bavaro blew a whistle. The former NFL great had short dark hair speckled with gray, and his big eyes seemed heavy from years of hard work. Another man stood behind Bavaro, taller and even wider.

Someone whispered, "That's Michael Strahan."

And it was. Ty took a deep breath and looked around

for a boy who looked like the famous Giants defensive end and thought he saw several candidates, boys so much taller and stronger looking than Ty that he wondered if this team really was just for twelve-year-olds. When he saw a boy with a gap in his teeth, Ty knew it was Michael Jr.

"Okay, guys," Bavaro said. "We've got some drills set up for you. There are about twenty receivers, and we'll keep just ten. We got five running backs and only room for two. Same thing with the defensive guys; we got about thirty and room for just ten, so don't feel bad if you don't make it. We've got some of the best kids in New Jersey, and we don't have much time to get this thing going. If you don't make it, I'm gonna suggest that someone get their dad to make up another team, and you'll probably whip our butts down in Miami. You just never know with this tryout stuff. Anyway, let's get going. Line up across this line here, and we'll get you warmed up."

Ty got on the line with the others and peered down the row of kids as they began doing high steps to loosen their hamstrings. He was the shortest, smallest kid there, and his spirits dropped. Once they had warmed up, though, Mark Bavaro had them line up on the sideline and sprint across in a race to see who was fastest. He kept removing the slower players, and after four tries, only Ty and three others were left.

"Who are you?" Bavaro asked Ty as he lined up

with the remaining kids.

"Ty Lewis."

"Oh, you're Tiger's kid brother. Yeah, he said you were fast. Okay, let's see. On your mark, set, go!"

Ty took off with the others. His legs seemed to fly and his feet barely to touch the turf. From the corner of his eye, he saw Strahan's son flying too. Ty ached to win. Something told him that if he didn't, he wasn't going to make this team. He was so much smaller, he knew he'd have to stand out as the fastest.

Ty leaned forward and dug deep for just a little more, some tiny reservoir of speed he hadn't tapped into yet.

CHAPTER SEVENTEEN

TY FOUND IT, JUST a spark, and he pulled away from the rest, ever so slightly, winning the race.

Bavaro made some notes on his clipboard, then looked up. "Okay, Lewis is our fastest man and you other three are right behind him, but the rest of you guys, don't worry. It's not always about speed. You got to be able to get open; that means being physical with the defensive backs. And then, most important of all, you gotta catch the ball. We can't win if we have guys who drop passes."

Mark Bavaro's son was named David. He was a thinner version of the father, but their faces were almost the same. David was tall for a twelve-year-old and he could throw the ball like a rocket launcher. A man Ty didn't recognize, but who he heard one of the kids whisper was a former Giants wide receivers' coach, gave them patterns to run. One thing the kids didn't have to worry about was catching a bad pass. David hit every receiver right in the hands, and Ty thought he knew why Bavaro senior wanted to get his son to the Super Bowl tournament. People would be impressed.

When Ty's turn came, the coach told him to run a twelve-yard post. Ty took off with automatic precision. Between games and practices, he'd run the pattern hundreds of times. He turned on his speed to impress both father and son. In his excitement, Ty forgot about the cut in his palm, so when the ball hit home, the shock of pain made him gasp and pull back. The ball skittered across the turf, and Ty shook his stinging hand like a wet rag.

He looked up only to see Bavaro shake his head and make a note on his clipboard. Ty retrieved the ball and examined his hand. Blood had soaked into the gauze. The ball must have split the skin wide open again. Ty wanted to show the former NFL star but remembered Agent Sutherland's words about Bavaro being old-school. He imagined Bavaro would not want to hear a kid whining about a cut on his hand. He'd never make the team if he complained.

They did a series of one-on-one drills with the defensive backs, running patterns and trying to get open. The defensive backs were quicker than anything Ty had seen in his ten games at Halpern Middle, and he wondered again if they could truly be just twelve years old. They knocked Ty and bumped him. When the ball got close, the defensive backs slapped it away. Ty knew he had to somehow get them to let him run a go route, just speed, straight down the field. He could dodge the first jam by the defensive cornerback and then leave him in the dust.

Instead of slumping toward the back of the line, Ty jogged right for the quarterback.

He stopped in front of David Bavaro. The quarterback blinked. Ty glanced around and lowered his voice.

"No matter what they tell me," Ty said, "next time I'm gonna run a go route. It's my only chance. Will you do it?"

"David!" the old player yelled. "Let's go!"

The young Bavaro gave only the slightest of nods. Ty wasn't sure whether he imagined it or not, but the next time he had a turn, he wiggled his cleats down into the turf, ready to take off like a rocket. The cornerback across from him settled his hips and let his arms hang loose. He wore a white sweatband and slick-looking black leather gloves. His limbs were knotted with muscles, and a vein pulsed in his neck.

"Give me ten yards square in," the receivers' coach said with a bark.

Ty swallowed and looked over at the quarterback, wondering if he'd throw it deep after the coach had called for a short pass.

"It's all or nothing." Ty spoke to himself, but the defensive back gave him a questioning look.

The quarterback barked the cadence, and Ty burst from his stance. The cornerback's hands sprang up like dueling mousetraps. Ty feinted one way and dodged back the other. One hand hit his shoulder and spun him slightly off balance, but Ty fell forward and was able to keep his feet. He dug in and churned forward. The effort at speed made his body ache, but the separation between him and the cornerback widened.

From the corner of his eye, Ty sensed the ball being launched far and deep, almost like a punt, almost too far for him to get to. Somehow, he did. As the ball fell, Ty stretched, wide open now. If he wanted even a chance of making it to Super Sunday, he had to make this catch. When the spinning leather bullet hit his hands, Ty saw sparks behind his eyelids and couldn't keep from hollering with pain.

CHAPTER EIGHTEEN

THE FBI CAR PULLED out of the Giants practice facility in the dark. Instead of sitting beside Sutherland, Ty got into the back, his head hung low. He almost didn't care about the mob anymore. Ty took a deep breath and let it out. Agent Sutherland's head shone like a boiled egg.

"Didn't you hear what he said about the guys who didn't make it forming another seven-on-seven team?" Agent Sutherland spoke over his shoulder. "You could play with them."

"They won't be the ones going to the Super Bowl in Miami," Ty said. "You need a big-time quarterback to win the qualifying tournament that gets you there, and that's David Bavaro. The other team won't even be worth lacing up my cleats for."

"Well, you tried."

Ty ground his teeth and flexed his stupid hand, remembering the day before and Sutherland snatching him from the hospital. "What the heck were you doing anyway, just showing up in Ian's car at the hospital last night?"

"Now it's my fault?" The agent spun his head all the way around to grimace at Ty. "No good deed goes unpunished, right? We make a decision to try and protect you, and I'm the bad guy? Come on, kid."

"I'm not your kid."

"You ran fast. You looked great."

"I dropped it."

"For a reason. Don't get down on yourself."

Ty sat silent with his arms folded. Agent Sutherland called someone and muttered into his phone, but Ty didn't listen. When they pulled to a stop in the driveway, Agent Sutherland hurried out and scanned the area.

"Don't worry, kid," the agent said as he followed Ty inside. "You won't have to see my face too much longer. When your brother gets back, I'll stay out in the car. Yeah, I called the doc on our way here. Thane's fever broke and he'll be getting out of ICU in the morning, so he's apt to be out in a day or two."

Ty had to smile at that news.

"I'm sorry," Ty said. "It's not your fault."

"That's part of my job, but I accept the apology." The agent set his briefcase down on the kitchen table.

"Really, you looked great out there. You run like greased lightning."

"Have you seen anyone who even looks like a mobster following us?"

"Happy to say I haven't."

"You want to have a soda or something?"

"You guys got a coffee machine?"

"Sure."

"That, I'll take."

Ty pointed at the machine on the kitchen countertop. Sutherland examined it, then pushed some buttons so that it crunched and whirred, and then a spring popped and hot coffee soon began to hiss into the pot. Ty took a sports drink from the fridge and turned on the big-screen TV in the great room, turning it to SportsCenter. Sutherland soon joined him with a steaming mug.

"How about that kid?" Sutherland raised his mug toward the TV, where Stuart Scott talked about some twelve-year-old who was supposedly helping the Falcons make their playoff run toward the Super Bowl. "You kinda look alike."

"I saw that the other day," Ty said. "They had his picture in the *Post*. I don't look like him, and I don't believe that 'football genius' stuff. They had a picture of Bigfoot in there one time, too."

"I don't know," Sutherland said. "You got the same shape face, something about the nose, and the same hair. Anyway, I heard your brother's team was signing him to a really big deal for next season, the football genius."

"Rumors." Ty flipped the channel to Discovery to watch a cave full of bats. "It's some stunt, that's all. His mom's in the Falcons PR department. My brother said that's probably where the whole thing came from."

"Teams use those tendencies, though, right?" Agent Sutherland said.

Ty turned up the volume as thousands of bats streaked across the jungle sky. "My brother studies the defensive formations so he can tell what coverage they're going to run. Some people say you can narrow down which plays an offense will run by a bunch of different things, like down and distance and formations and field position and all that, but they use computers to figure that out. That kid is my age."

Ty fished the cell phone from his pocket. "I'm going to order a pizza. What do you like? Pepperoni?"

"Sounds good."

As he wrapped up his order, Ty got a call waiting on his phone. He didn't recognize the number, but knew it was a New Jersey area code. His heart pumped fast. Would the Blade or Pete Bonito call him up?

Ty looked at the FBI agent, then clicked over.

"Ty Lewis?"

Ty swallowed. "Yes."

"This is Mark Bavaro."

CHAPTER NINETEEN

TY'S FACE FELT HOT. He knew he hadn't made the team, but it was somehow more painful to have to hear the news from the former star player.

"Hello," Ty said.

"Listen," Bavaro said, "you got great speed. You remind me of your brother."

Ty flexed his injured hand and felt the words building up in his throat and he had to say them. "I can catch better than I did. I've got great hands. I just . . . had a bad day. Really."

Bavaro began to chuckle.

"Why is that funny?" Ty was unable to keep the annoyance out of his tone, even though Bavaro was a football legend.

"I saw the blood all over your bandage. I thought it

was pretty cool that you didn't even say anything about it. That had to hurt, right?"

"Pretty much," Ty said, feeling better about being laughed at.

"I heard you had good hands. Caught a bunch of passes for your team this season, right?"

"Sixty-seven."

"Nice. So. Okay, normally you got good hands?"

"I really do."

"But tough enough not to whine about it," Bavaro said. "And fast as—"

"Greased lightning?" Ty burst out.

Bavaro laughed. "So, you want to be on the Raptors? There's gonna be a lot of long, hard practices."

Ty's heart pounded wildly. Excitement rushed into his chest. "You bet I do."

"Great. We start tomorrow, back at the Giants facility. Seven thirty."

"Thanks, Coach Bavaro," Ty said. "I'll be there."

Ty hung up the phone and grinned at Agent Sutherland. "I really did it."

"No excuses."

Ty's smile faded. "My brother will be happy. If he hadn't told the doctor, there's no way I would have gone."

"He's a good brother."

"He's everything. You know these guys, Bennie the Blade and Bonito? I'm scared of them, but the thing that scares me most is them doing something to Thane."

"Who's Thane?"

"My brother, Tiger. I call him Thane. That's his name."

Tiger was what most people called Thane, but it still sounded funny to him because his brother always insisted that Ty call him by the name their parents had given him, even if it was a bit unusual.

Sutherland's face grew serious. "You'll be fine, Ty. Your uncle will be in and out of town by Thursday, and I'll be watching you the whole time. We're not worried about them getting at your brother. It's *you* we're pretty sure they're talking about."

Ty nodded and turned his attention back to the cave bats on TV. The pizza came. They ate and watched a college basketball game before Ty turned on the ten o'clock news. When the sports anchor led off his broadcast with news about Tiger Lewis's hospitalization, Ty sat on the edge of his seat.

"Oh, no," Agent Sutherland said. "You've got to be kidding me."

The agent pulled a phone from his pocket and hit a speed dial.

"What?" Ty said. "He's saying Thane should get out the day after tomorrow. That's great news. It means it really must be true."

Agent Sutherland seemed not to be paying attention. Instead, he spoke into the phone.

"Sutherland here. Yes. No. Did anyone see the news?

I thought we had a lid on that. No, everything is fine, it's just I thought the hospital agreed not to say where he was one way or another."

Ty could just hear the buzz of a voice on the other end as Sutherland listened.

"I still think—" Sutherland shook his head in frustration. "Of course I can handle it. I thought we should take precautions, that's all. Yes. I understand. No, sir. Good night."

Sutherland tucked the phone back into his pocket.

"What's wrong?" Ty asked.

Sutherland looked at the TV for a moment, then sighed. "They weren't supposed to be giving out any information."

"They didn't talk about me."

"Well, if the mob hears your brother is in the hospital, they'll know the best chance to get to you is during all the confusion," the agent said. "You don't want them knowing anything they don't already know. Anyway, I asked for some backup on the street."

"Oh." Ty didn't know what else to say. He shut off the TV. "Well, I guess I'm going to go up to bed."

"You sure are used to being on your own," the agent said, forcing a laugh. "I got nieces and nephews, and they'd stay up all night if my sister didn't make them go to bed. I'm impressed."

"I've got to do well in school," Ty said. "My brother always talks about that. And he says that you need to get sleep if you want to be good in school and especially to be a good football player. I want to be both, so it's just something I learned to do."

"You're definitely older than your age." Sutherland stood and headed for the kitchen table. "Okay, I'll be right here, so no worries."

"You don't have to stay awake all night, Agent Sutherland. I'll put the alarm on, and that's a big couch."

"Don't worry about me."

"Okay. I'll see you in the morning." Ty went upstairs and got ready for bed. On his desk sat the computer. Ty was afraid to even turn it on, let alone get on Facebook. He felt like the computer somehow connected him with the mob, and that once he turned it on, they'd know his every move. He was happy to have the big FBI agent downstairs, but even so, sleep didn't come easy.

There was lots to worry about.

Ty had no idea of the time when he awoke. All he knew was that there had been a tremendous crash. Ty peeked out from beneath his covers. Only the faintest light spilling into the room from the stars gave ghosts of shape to the furniture, closet, and clothes on the floor.

The door to his room swung slowly open.

Ty gasped, unable to move or even breathe as the dark shape of a man stepped inside and stood hovering over his bed.

CHAPTER TWENTY

TY FELT THE SCREAM jammed up in his throat.

"You okay?" It was Sutherland, hunched over, ready for a fight.

"What are you doing?" Ty asked.

"Did you hear that?"

"That crash?" Ty asked.

"Sh." Sutherland moved to the window, gun in his hand, and opened a seam in the curtains. "There's a ladder down there in the grass, right below your window."

Ty shivered.

Sutherland stood straight and dialed his phone. After a moment, he said, "What's going on out there? Did you guys see something?"

Ty heard the buzz of a voice on the other end.

Finally Sutherland said, "Okay, keep going. I'll stay here with the kid, but let me know."

"What is it?" Ty asked.

Sutherland flipped on the light in the corner. "They were here. They must have come through the back. I had two guys on the street. They said they were sitting there keeping an eye out for a vehicle when one of them happened to look at the house and saw someone with a ladder. They got out and started running for the house, but whoever it was saw them. He ditched the ladder and ran."

"Who? Bennie the Blade?"

"Maybe it was." Sutherland muttered, as if talking to himself, before he said, "They're gone now, though. Don't worry."

"Some professional killer just tried to break into my room, and I'm not supposed to worry?" Ty's voice rose like howling wind. "You said I'd be okay."

"You are, aren't you?"

Ty sat up in bed and looked down at his hands. "Yes."

"See? They're not going to just try and sneak in your window again. They know now."

"Know what?" Ty asked.

"That we'll be watching the front, the back, and everywhere in between until your uncle is out of town. Once that happens, you'll be completely safe. We were right about their code. Your uncle is definitely the cake they've been talking about. I'll let you get back to sleep, buddy. Don't worry, I'll be down there."

"Sleep? I can't sleep."

"You said you could before."

"That was before someone tried to come into my window and grab me." Ty stared at Sutherland until the agent turned up his hands and shrugged.

"This is crazy," Ty said.

"Don't worry. I got you. This is what we do. You couldn't be any safer."

The agent closed the door as he left, but his words didn't help. Ty lay awake, tossing and turning, until finally he cracked open his copy of *The Giver* and read about a boy who—like Ty—found himself alone and scared. Before he knew it, he awoke with the book open on his chest and the alarm clock beeping. He got up and ready for school, stepping cautiously down the stairs until he heard the toaster ding and Agent Sutherland humming to himself in the kitchen.

"Did you talk to the doctor?" Ty asked.

The agent jumped. "Wow. Kid. You can't sneak up on me like that."

"Did you talk to the doctor?" Ty asked again, unable to read the agent's expression.

"Yes," Sutherland said, "I did."

CHAPTER TWENTY-ONE

AGENT SUTHERLAND BROKE INTO a grin. "Good news. Your brother turned the corner. The fever stayed down last night. He'll be out of ICU today, and they're letting him come home tomorrow for sure."

"Can I go see him?" Ty didn't try to hide his excitement.

"We'll head over there before school. I figured toast and peanut butter." The agent set two plates down on the table next to the glasses of orange juice he'd already poured. "My nephew loves it. Lots of protein."

Ty slammed down his breakfast and threw his things together for school, eager to see Thane. He rode in the front seat with Sutherland, who continued to check the rearview mirror and look all around at any stoplights. Even though Ty knew it was the man's job, it still made him nervous. Sutherland parked right in front of the hospital's doors and got out with his briefcase. The agent had a talk with the security guard about leaving the car in a no-parking zone, showing the guard his badge before they walked right in.

Thane sat propped up in the same bed Ty had last seen him in and with what looked like the same IV dripping into the vein in his arm. He smiled weakly at Ty, looking pale and tired. Ty rushed into the room and hugged his brother tight. Thane rubbed the back of Ty's head, pulling Ty in to his chest.

When his brother let go, Ty stood back and said, "I don't want to bang your knee again."

Thane waved his hand in the air. "That had nothing to do with me getting an infection. It happens. Sometimes things happen. There doesn't always have to be someone to blame, you know."

"I know," Ty said. "Thane, this is Agent Sutherland."

Thane noticed the agent for the first time. "Agent?"

Sutherland held out his hand. "FBI. Big Jets fan, Tiger. Pleasure to meet you."

"What's wrong?" Thane asked.

Sutherland took a deep breath. He turned to close the door behind him before telling Thane everything he knew, and everything that had happened.

"Here." The agent removed the folder from his briefcase and showed Thane the pictures of Pete Bonito and Bennie the Blade.

The pictures had the opposite effect on Thane than they had with Ty. Thane's brow wrinkled and his mouth twisted into a snarl.

"So, what are we going to do?" Thane asked, his pasty skin seeming to grow even paler.

"It'll be me and a couple other agents, now, watching Ty around the clock until your uncle gets in and out of town. Ty should be perfectly safe."

"I've heard that before," Thane said. "Would he have been perfectly safe last night if they didn't drop their ladder?"

Sutherland's red face glowed. "It all worked out okay."

Thane sat up straighter in the bed. "The FBI has been telling us for months that we weren't in any danger. I don't call someone trying to break into my brother's bedroom window safe. You didn't even go after them."

"They were gone," the agent said. "Even if we had a manhunt, what were we going to charge them with? Technically, they hadn't done anything more than trespass."

"FBI," Thane said with disgust. "That stands for 'Famous But Incompetent,' right?"

Now it was Sutherland's turn to scowl. "All due respect, Tiger. It wasn't me—or anyone else in the FBI—who decided to give inside information to the D'Amico family so they could cash in on the Jets games, was it?"

CHAPTER TWENTY-TWO

"MY LITTLE BROTHER THOUGHT it was for some fantasy football website," Thane said, his voice rising.

Ty cringed at the sound of the words that so often ran through his mind. Their Uncle Gus had told Ty exactly what Thane just said, that the information Ty got from his older brother would be used for nothing more than a fantasy football website. Ty had known it wasn't technically right for him to pass on explicit injury information on the Jets players, but the temptation of being able to play football had been just too much for him.

Agent Sutherland scratched furiously at his bald head. "Whatever anyone thought, *you* two created this problem."

Thane closed his mouth and rolled up his lower lip.

Finally, he nodded his head.

"You're right," he said.

Sutherland's expression softened. "Last night was crazy, but thank God everything worked out. Honestly, with our presence, these guys will stay away from Ty. I imagine they'll spend their time trying to figure out another way to get to your uncle."

"Is our uncle safe?" Thane asked.

"The US Marshals are pretty darn good," Sutherland said.

Thane sat, absorbing the information, the lines in his face beginning to fade. "Okay, well, I'm in here until tomorrow, so don't you guys let Ty out of your sight for a second."

"We got him, Tiger," Sutherland said, nodding at Ty. "Like I said, around the clock. He'll be fine."

They stayed and talked, Ty telling Thane all about the Raptors and how he'd made it.

"Let me see that cut," Thane said.

Ty held out his hand, and Thane looked proudly at Agent Sutherland and said, "How about that?"

"Tough enough to be a Jet himself one day, right?" Sutherland said.

"I'll say," Thane said.

Ty felt his face warm and he looked down at the floor.

"Listen." Thane let go of Ty's hand and pointed at it. "You want to put a lot of ointment on that, then put some no-stick gauze pads, *then* tape it up good, first with stretch tape, then the stuff they use on ankles. The big thing is to keep it soft and slippery on the inside of the tape job. It's not going to take away the pain completely, but it'll help."

"Advice from an NFL star," Sutherland said to Ty. "You can't beat that."

They talked about the details of the tournament, how if the Raptors won, the two of them would be making a trip to Miami.

"You should go down there," Ty said to Agent Sutherland, feeling bad about him being left out of the excitement. The agent nodded his head like that would be a good idea, but said nothing.

After a few more minutes of talking about the beach and sunshine, the Sea aquarium, and riding WaveRunners out on the ocean, Thane began to look tired.

"I'll stop back after school," Ty said.

"Then you get to that practice," Thane said.

Ty kissed his brother, and Agent Sutherland took him to school. After a day that seemed to go on forever, Ty finally broke free and found Sutherland waiting. As promised, Ty visited Thane again. His older brother actually made the nurses get a bunch of tape and bandages so he could personally tape up Ty's hand. Ty went to practice full of confidence. Maybe it was the excitement of how well he did at 7-on-7 practice or Agent Sutherland's reassuring words, but whatever the reason, Ty had no trouble sleeping that night.

When Ty woke up Thursday, he went downstairs and watched the morning news with Agent Sutherland while he ate breakfast. Halfway through a bagel with cream cheese, the newscaster began to talk about the grand jury testimony and how the US Marshals had Gus Slatz under heavy guard.

CHAPTER TWENTY-THREE

A PRETTY, DARK-HAIRED WOMAN in a gray pantsuit spoke to the camera in front of the columns of the federal courthouse.

"Government prosecutors are saying that additional testimony they expect today from Gus Slatz could put an end to the D'Amico crime family for good. As a result, authorities have kept Slatz hidden under lock and key. He's expected to arrive here at this courthouse around ten o'clock this morning in an armored vehicle. That's right, an armored vehicle. That's how seriously the government is taking the safety of this key witness."

Ty looked at Agent Sutherland, who winked at him.

"Looks like I'm almost in the clear," Ty said.

"I'd have to say so," Sutherland said. "Let's not count our chickens yet, though. I'll be a lot more comfortable when I know your uncle is on a plane back to wherever it is they moved him to."

"When will that be?" Ty asked.

Sutherland shrugged. "Only the marshals know. Maybe this evening?"

School dragged by. Every time Ty looked at the clock, he thought about his Uncle Gus testifying to the grand jury. He knew Uncle Gus had to be scared silly. Lucy Catalone had terrified Uncle Gus even before the mobsters wanted him dead. Ty could only imagine how bad it was for Uncle Gus knowing these dangerous men were even more eager to see him gone.

Before practice, Ty had Agent Sutherland take him home for a snack and to change. Ty put on his computer and went to the *New York Times* website, where he saw a story posted only twelve minutes earlier. The headline read GUS SLATZ SINKS MOB.

"Wow," Ty said, reading on about how his uncle's testimony resulted in seventeen more indictments against Lucy Catalone and Al D'Amico.

"Yeah," Sutherland said, looking over Ty's shoulder. "It went well. The agency is pretty happy."

Ty felt a mixture of excitement and fear. He was excited because the danger seemed to be over but scared because everything that had happened in the last couple days felt like a brush with death.

Practice started early, so Ty had to tape his own hand with the encouragement of Agent Sutherland, who stopped at a drugstore and bought a bag of supplies.

Coach Bavaro ran them relentlessly. They ran pattern after pattern, footballs flying through the air. In the final session of practice, they scrimmaged against their own defense. Ty lined up as the outside receiver and read the defense in front of him. It looked like a single safety defense, probably cover three. That meant Ty should break off his route at about fifteen yards and run a comeback.

David Bavaro began the cadence, and just as the ball snapped, the defense shifted. Ty read it on the run, seeing that what they really were doing was playing two deep safeties. That would leave a cornerback underneath to intercept the comeback. Ty got to fifteen yards and, instead of coming back, he veered toward the middle of the field on a skinny post pattern. David Bavaro saw him and delivered the pass in a long, high arc, dropping it perfectly into his hands.

Ty caught it and ran into the end zone, untouched.

He jogged back to the huddle to find both Bavaros, coach and son, grinning and slapping his back.

"You read it on the run," Coach Bavaro said. "Great job, Ty. That's hard to learn."

David Bavaro said, "I knew you were going to do it. I threw it before you even made the break."

"Now that's the kind of chemistry that'll get us to Miami!" Coach Bavaro grabbed both boys and hugged them to his chest.

Ty's face blazed with pride and a little bit of embarrassment. He couldn't wait to tell his brother.

CHAPTER TWENTY-FOUR

THE EXCITEMENT OF THANE coming home made Ty nearly forget about Uncle Gus and the grand jury testimony. He ran inside from practice to give his brother a hug and tell him excitedly about the chemistry he was creating with David Bavaro.

"That's great." Thane beamed proudly from his place on the couch.

"Well," Agent Sutherland said, checking his watch, "your uncle is probably stepping onto an airplane right now and on his way back to Timbuktu or wherever they've got him. You guys have absolutely nothing to worry about anymore."

"What about when Uncle Gus comes back?" Ty asked.

Sutherland raised his eyebrows, and the wrinkles on his forehead climbed up toward the top of his bald head. "For the trial? That won't be for a year or more. These things take a long time, and a lot can change. By then, D'Amico's nephew might not even want to get his uncle back. So I guess this is good-bye."

"Agent Sutherland," Thane said, starting to rise.

"No, don't get up."

Thane sat back into the pillows on the couch. "I just want you to know how much I appreciate you looking after Ty."

"First of all, it's my job," the agent said, handing Thane a business card. "But he's a good kid. I think you know that."

"I do."

Ty shook Sutherland's hand.

"You call me if you guys need anything," Sutherland said to Thane before heading for the door. "My cell number is on there. And stay away from that Facebook page, will you?"

Ty looked down.

"Agent Sutherland?" Thane said. "About Miami. I've got a couple tickets for the Super Bowl. If you can get down there, I'd be happy to give them to you."

Sutherland stopped and turned around, the gold tooth glinting from his smile. "You don't have to do that. Really. I appreciate it, but I don't think I can accept it."

"You really should. They don't cost me anything. I want you to have them."

The agent nodded his head. "I tell you what, if you

let me pay you face value for them, I'd love to take them. They cost ten times that much from a ticket broker, so it'd still be a big favor."

"Done."

"Great. Thank you, Tiger."

Thane held up the agent's card. "I'll have them delivered to you at this address, and you can mail me a check. Maybe we'll see you down there. If this Seven-on-Seven thing goes well for Ty, at least one of us will be playing in Miami."

When the agent had gone, Ty and his brother watched TV for a while until Thane started to fall asleep. Ty helped him with his crutches, and the two of them went upstairs. Thane got into bed and took some pain pills, thanking Ty for his help and reminding him to put the alarm on. Ty went into the hallway between their two rooms and armed the system. The buttons chirped as he punched in the code, a combination of his football jersey number and Thane's. That done, he used the shower and climbed into bed himself.

It felt good to have Thane back, and Ty stretched in his bed and broke open his book, reading until his eyes drooped. He turned out the light, sighed with comfort, and rolled onto his side.

When he heard the chirp of the alarm buttons, his eyes shot open. Then he remembered Thane was home. He let the air out of his lungs and closed his eyes to go back to sleep. A moment later, his eyes shot open again. The thought of Thane struggling by himself with crutches down the stairs to get something to eat made Ty raise his covers and climb out of bed. He reached for the robe on the back of his door and tugged it on.

Before he could tie it shut, Ty heard the sound of footsteps coming *up* the stairs. His brain spun in confusion. Thane hadn't had time to get down and already be coming back up, and Ty would have heard the sound of his crutches. The footsteps moving up the stairs sounded soft.

Ty's heart jumped into his throat. He froze in panic, unable to move as he heard whoever it was sneak past his bedroom door, heading down the hall to where Thane slept. Ty heard heavy breathing and peeked around the edge of his door.

He peered down the dark hallway and gasped at what he saw.

CHAPTER TWENTY-FIVE

BEFORE THE CHRISTMAS BREAK, *Ty's health teacher, Mrs. Hoeft, had given the class a big project for their emergency unit. Ty and the rest of his classmates had to—among other things—create an emergency exit map for their homes. After hearing about how many people died in their own homes from fire, Ty took the project very seriously and explored the big mansion for the best ways out, especially from his and Thane's bedrooms. Thane's escape route was easy. A balcony overlooking the back lawn and the hills beyond gave easy access to the terrace and the grass below.*

Ty's route hadn't been as easy to decide on. There were several ways he could go, including through Thane's bedroom. But, if there was a real fire, and a bad one, Ty decided his best chance would be to hang from his window and drop down onto a narrow roof covering the front entrance of the house. From there, he could hang from a copper gutter and drop down into the bushes without hurting himself. The tricky part was the first drop and making sure he didn't simply fall from the roof. That would get him hurt.

So, with extreme danger afoot in the hallway, and who knew what other perils in the house below, Ty found himself halfway out his bedroom window before he even took another breath. When he did pause, he did so in shame. Pete Bonito and Bennie the Blade— or whoever was in the house—scared him. But hadn't he always told himself that losing his brother would be worse than harm coming to himself? That's what he had thought, but here he was with his brother in danger, and he was running for the exit.

Something flooded his chest. Courage? Insanity? Love? Ty didn't know; he only knew that it propelled him back into the room and made him scoop up the Yankees bat given to Thane by Derek Jeter in exchange for a Jets helmet. The bat was the real thing, but it felt surprisingly light in Ty's grip. He swept open his bedroom door and looked before stepping into the dark hallway.

The thick, short shape of a hunched-over man had his hand on the doorknob to Thane's room. He wore a bulky parka and a knit cap and he eased the door open and took one step into the room. Ty bolted toward the man with a gasp.

The sound made the dark shape spin around and cry out. The sound made Ty's insides melt.

The man launched himself at Ty.

Ty reared back and swung the bat.

CHAPTER TWENTY-SIX

TY CONNECTED WITH SOMETHING. The man yelped and fell at Ty's feet, but his hands grasped Ty's ankles and locked on in a death grip. Ty swung the bat again.

Klunk.

The man collapsed in a pile.

Thane burst from his bedroom on crutches, wearing only boxer shorts. He flipped on the light and blinked. "What?"

Ty stepped out of the man's loose grip, trembling. He held the bat out to Thane until his older brother took it.

The shape on the floor looked familiar to Ty, but the thick clothes and cap hid his identity. Thane nudged the man with his toe. The man lay still.

"Holy moly." Thane set his crutches against the railing, bent down over the man, pulled off his cap, and rolled him onto his back.

Ty blinked and thought he might scream.

The sound caught in his throat and became a useless gurgle.

Thane looked up at Ty. "Uncle Gus?"

CHAPTER TWENTY-SEVEN

TY COULD ONLY NOD his head yes.

It was Uncle Gus. He looked thinner, and the bags under his eyes were darker than Ty remembered. His greasy hair had been cut and dyed a color somewhere between orange and yellow. A thin dribble of blood trickled down Uncle Gus's mouth, and his nose twitched like a rabbit's.

"Did I kill him?" Ty's voice shook.

There was a part of Ty that despised Uncle Gus. His uncle was mean and greedy. He'd put Ty to work like a slave, scrubbing toilets and mopping kitchens in the grubbiest of places for his former cleaning business. Worst of all, Uncle Gus's greed had put not only Thane's career in danger, but also his health and well-being. Still, in the end, Uncle Gus had sided with the good guys and had put his own life at risk by agreeing to testify against the D'Amico mob.

Thane knelt down on his good knee and gently slapped Uncle Gus's cheek. "You dinged him pretty good. I think he hit his face when he fell, but I think he'll be okay."

"He's bleeding."

"Just a little."

The thin trickle of blood continued to flow from Uncle Gus's nose.

"Uncle Gus," Thane said, shaking him.

Uncle Gus's eyes popped open. He grasped his ribs and groaned.

"What are you doing here?" Ty asked. "You're supposed to be hiding."

"I gave them the slip," Uncle Gus said, sitting up, grinning, and dabbing at the blood on his upper lip.

"They had you in an armored car," Ty said, remembering the newscast from that morning.

"Sure," Uncle Gus said. "They were protecting *me*. They weren't ready for me to give *them* the slip. It was easy. We were at Teterboro Airport, all ready to get onto a plane, and I asked to use the bathroom. They were covering the outside so no one could get in at me. I just went down the hall and out the back door. I ran out into the street and caught a cab dropping someone off. By the time they realized it, I was gone."

Uncle Gus began to giggle and snort, then he winced

and touched his nose again. "Ow. I had to see you, Tiger."

"Me?" Thane poked a finger into his own chest. "Why?"

Uncle Gus licked his lips. "I kind of need a loan."

"A loan?"

"Money."

"Uncle Gus, you're in a witness protection program," Thane said. "The government pays for everything."

"Not exactly everything." Uncle Gus's eyes shifted back and forth between Thane and Ty. "There are a few creature comforts they just don't understand. I mean, TV isn't TV unless you've got a big screen, and the games aren't fun to watch if you can't bet a little something on them."

Thane gave Ty a look to signal his disgust and shook his head as if to say that some people never learned.

"I need some help, Tiger." Uncle Gus began to whine. "Just till I can get things cranked up again. The jobs they get me? Ugh. Canning fish? Sorting mail? I need to get on my feet. I need some breathing room."

"Do you want me to talk to the FBI people or the US Marshals?" Thane asked, taking up his crutches.

Uncle Gus staggered to his feet with Ty's help, clutching his ribs and breathing heavy.

"No." Uncle Gus's face turned sullen. His lower lip stuck out. "I risk my life to save you and Ty, and I can't get a loan?"

Ty wanted to scream out that if it weren't for Uncle Gus and his gambling and his greed, no one's life would have been at risk. He could tell by the look on Thane's face that his older brother was actually thinking about giving him the money.

"I've got a little girl—your cousin, who treated Ty like a brother—who can't even afford a new dress." Uncle Gus clasped his hands. "Okay, forget about me, but can't you help me out even a little for my family? I'm not talking about much."

Ty looked at Thane and shook his head slightly back and forth. He seriously doubted Charlotte wanted a new dress that Uncle Gus couldn't afford.

"How much?" Thane asked.

Uncle Gus licked his lips again. "Ten thousand, and I'm good for a long time."

Thane's mouth fell open. "Ten *thousand*?"

CHAPTER TWENTY-EIGHT

UNCLE GUS BLINKED AND spoke softly. "Tiger, how can you look at me like that? Your signing bonus was seven and a half *million*. That's like me giving some bum a five-dollar bill for lunch. Ten thousand is nothing to you."

Thane pressed his lips tight together, and his face turned color. "Ten thousand dollars is a lot to anyone, Uncle Gus. But I can help you."

"You'll be helping little Charlotte." Uncle Gus nodded like a Sunday school teacher as he uttered his daughter's name.

"Come on, Uncle Gus." Thane led them all downstairs on his crutches. He slumped down at the desk in his office, took a checkbook out of the drawer, and wrote out a check for their uncle.

Uncle Gus examined the check and sniffed, wiping

his eyes. "Made out to 'cash.' Perfect. My bank will make me wait a few days until it clears, but it'll do for sure. It's only a loan, my boy. I will pay it back."

"No, Uncle Gus." Thane struggled up on his crutches and patted Uncle Gus on the back. "You probably won't, and I don't want you to worry about it. I'm happy to help, but you can't do this again. You've got to make this last and work at whatever job they get you."

Uncle Gus stood straighter and stuffed the check into his pocket. "I'm ready to serve my country, even if it means my own hardship. You've done a good deed, son."

The three of them moved through the great room and into the kitchen.

"Don't you think the marshals are looking for you? Won't they be mad?" Ty finally felt he could ask the questions that had been bugging him.

Uncle Gus broke out in a sly grin. "They look kind of stupid, not keeping me under guard. All I have to do is call, and they'll be glad they got their package again. That's all I am to those guys. Do you believe they wouldn't even buy me a cigar? Me, the star witness. They'll come get me and be glad if we stay quiet about it, the buffoons."

"Won't they be mad, though?" Ty asked, not wanting to say who he thought the real buffoon was.

"Mad? I'm the one who's mad." Uncle Gus jabbed a thumb into his big gut. "Can you believe they're making us move again? Wait till I find out what that's all about. You can bet I'll raise some storm clouds over that one."

Ty looked away for a moment, feeling guilty about the Facebook.

Uncle Gus patted the pocket where the check was and smiled. "But my trip to see you boys is going to help ease the pain, thanks to your big brother. We'll have food on the table now, and clothes on our backs."

Ty rolled his eyes.

"You don't look too skinny to me," Thane said, unable to keep from smiling.

Uncle Gus's eyes got big and shiny, and he looked up at Thane. "You can't imagine the food they expect us to eat. Chuck steaks. Hamburger! Nothing prime. You know I've always enjoyed a sirloin. If I'd known how shabbily we'd be treated, I have to say I . . . Well, of course I'd do it because I'm helping put those criminals where they belong."

Ty shook his head in real disgust, not believing a word of it.

"Can I use your phone?" Uncle Gus asked.

"Right there next to the fridge," Thane said.

"And, maybe a libation?" Uncle Gus reached tentatively for the fridge.

"Libation?" Ty looked at his older brother.

"A drink," Thane said.

"Not just any drink," Uncle Gus said.

"I don't have any beer, Uncle Gus," Thane said.

Uncle Gus's shoulders slumped, and his hand dropped away from the fridge. "Game Day Light. You ever hear of that?"

"It's the beer you can get at Seven-Eleven?" Thane said.

"I never thought I'd meet a beer I didn't like," Uncle Gus said. "It's pathetic. I ask for beer and they give me that. I'm putting these ruthless killers behind bars, and they give me Game Day Light? My ribs are killing me."

"Your nose stopped bleeding," Thane said, angling his head for a view of Uncle Gus's nose.

"Can I get some aspirin anyway?" Uncle Gus asked.

"Corner cupboard," Thane said.

Uncle Gus took his aspirin and called the US Marshals. Ty heard shouting on the other end of the line. Then they all sat down on the couch with Uncle Gus to wait.

"You two go back to bed," he said. "I wouldn't have come here in the middle of the night like this if I had my old life."

Uncle Gus sighed.

"I'm sorry it's so bad, Uncle Gus," Thane said.

Uncle Gus patted his pocket again. "You've lightened the load, Tiger. You've done a good deed."

When the government car pulled into the driveway, Uncle Gus slouched out to meet the marshals. The two men—dressed in dark suits, with short haircuts—gestured wildly and raised their voices. Ty and Thane watched from the front door. Ty thought he heard them call Uncle Gus a fool.

"That's a lot of money," Ty said as the car pulled out of the driveway.

"I couldn't not help him," Thane said. "Especially after you walloped him. How did he get the code to turn off the alarm?"

"Could Charlotte have told him? She knows the code," Ty said. "He must have tricked her. That's all I can think of."

"He is tricky."

Ty bit his tongue in order not to criticize Thane for being tricked himself, out of a ten-thousand-dollar check.

"I mean, he gave the US Marshals the slip, right? Unbelievable." Thane patted Ty on the head before returning his grip to the crutches. "Come on, let's get back to bed."

"I don't know if I can even sleep." Ty looked at his hands, which still trembled.

"Come on," Thane said, thumping up the stairs. "Sleep in my room."

"With your knee? No, I'll be all right."

"You can sleep on the floor. You won't bump me there."

Ty helped Thane get a couple of pillows under his knee and got him a drink so he could take some more pain pills. Thane's throat bulged as he swallowed down the fat white pills. He handed the water glass back to Ty and asked for two more pillows. Ty went down the hall to his own room, taking some extra pillows from his bed as well as his own blankets. Thane looked grateful as Ty gently raised his leg and propped it on the pillows.

Exhaustion settled in on Ty, and he lay down on some blankets on the floor beside Thane's bed. He listened as his brother shifted in the bed above him.

"You okay?"

"Aches a little is all," Thane said, sounding groggy.

"You want more pillows?"

"No, you did good."

Ty listened for more sounds of discomfort and after a minute thought his brother might have nodded off.

"Thane?"

"What's up?"

"Do you think that's the last we'll ever see him?"

"Uncle Gus?"

"Yeah," Ty said, rolling onto his side and looking out the window. The faint glow from a nearby streetlamp lit up little starbursts of ice frozen on the glass.

"I think Uncle Gus and all those other problems are over," Thane said.

"For good, really?"

"Really."

Ty felt a sudden chill because he knew without doubt that his brother was wrong.

CHAPTER TWENTY-NINE

DESPITE THE WINTER COLD, sun shone down through the gray clouds into Giants Stadium. The Raptors had cut through the competition all day long, but now, in the finals, they were down 30–35 to a team from Trenton. Only two seconds remained.

"Okay," Mark Bavaro said, one arm draped around his son's shoulders, the other around Ty's as he leaned into the huddle. "They're going to be in a deep zone, so they'll be waiting for you, but we can do this. Just like we practiced it. Trips left scramble, sienna short, deep vertical. Got it?"

The steam of their coach's breath drifted toward the sky. Everyone nodded.

The former Giants star started to leave the huddle, but pulled Ty aside before jogging off the field. "You've got the speed. All you have to do is make the catch, and we go to Miami. You can do it."

Ty looked up into the former NFL player's big, sleepy eyes and saw the fire inside that must have been part of what made him so great. For the past week and a half, Ty had admired the former player's quiet intensity. Without ever yelling, Bavaro not only inspired the team, but there was also something a bit scary about him that made the players hang on every word he said and respect every instruction he gave. In many ways, Bavaro reminded Ty of his own brother. So when the former player said Ty could do it, Ty couldn't help but believe.

David Bavaro winked at Ty and called the play again, breaking the huddle. The Raptors wore blood-red T-shirts over long-sleeved Under Armour shirts with matching knit caps to keep their ears from freezing off. Ty jogged to the line and studied the deep zone defense. The play called for the other three receivers to use up three of the deep defenders with decoy routes and for the running back to distract the underneath coverage on Ty's side of the field. The intent was to isolate the deep man on Ty's side of the field in a one-on-one situation so that Ty could use his speed to break free. There wasn't really a second target for the quarterback to throw to. Ty had to get open if they were to win. It was all or nothing.

Ty took a deep breath, huffed into his cold hands, and looked up into the stands. Thane sat with a couple of the Jets players who'd come to watch and cheer. Thane gave Ty a thumbs-up. Ty nodded and wiggled his feet into the turf to get a good start. David Bavaro began the cadence, and the defense shifted. Ty realized that number twenty-two, Trenton's best cornerback, had switched spots with a teammate to put himself on Ty's quadrant of the field.

Twenty-two was taller and faster than his teammates. His best skills, however, were his reactions. When he'd covered Ty earlier in the contest, Ty noticed that twenty-two could read Ty's eyes and hands and would only look back for the ball when Ty's eyes and hands told him it was coming. This kind of advanced reaction gave twenty-two the best chance for an interception or to break up the pass, something he'd done plenty of so far in this game. Ty ignored the drop of doubt that plunked into his mind. He coiled his muscles and shot forward on the count. Ty didn't see the other defenders, or his teammates. His focus was completely on twenty-two.

Ty tore straight down the field, and twenty-two started to back up. When Ty got even with him, twenty-two swiveled his hips and tried to match strides. David Bavaro launched the ball. Ty read its trajectory and threw out his hands to make the catch. Twenty-two read it perfectly. His hand extended with Ty's and his head swung around to watch the pass.

The coverage was flawless.

CHAPTER THIRTY

THE INSTANT TWENTY-TWO SPUN his head around to watch the pass, Ty dropped his own hands and put on a fresh surge of speed. With his hands down, and twenty-two's up in the air, Ty pulled away from him. Twenty-two realized, too late, that the pass would fall well beyond the spot where Ty had raised his hands to catch it. Twenty-two dropped his own hands and angled his head forward in a desperate attempt to catch up.

He was too late.

Ty was the faster man and was a step ahead. He extended his hands once again, stretching his fingers, with the ball falling fast. He felt the leather, squeezed with his fingers, and held on. Just as Ty secured the ball, twenty-two dove and swung a hand, clipping Ty's foot. Ty spun and fell forward.

In the air, he tucked the ball under one arm and planted his free hand on the turf. His feet caught up. He replanted his hand, gaining balance. One more plant and he regained his feet, sprinting into the end zone. Ty turned to see twenty-two looking up at him from where he lay on the turf. Ty's teammates jumped up and down, and David Bavaro sprinted the length of the field to hug him and hold him up in the air. Ty looked up into the stands to see his brother slapping high fives with his Jets teammates.

Mark Bavaro burst into the middle of the players and hugged both his son and Ty.

"We did it! We did it!" Bavaro screamed, and laughed wildly.

The teams shook hands, and Ray Anderson, the NFL's executive vice president, presented the Raptors with a four-foot trophy, along with an invitation to the NFL's Super Bowl 7-on-7 Tournament. A photographer from the Newark *Star-Ledger* snapped off pictures of the team and the trophy. Ty stayed in the back, unconcerned when someone's shoulder blocked half his face from the shot.

Outside, Ty got another hug from his brother. Thane still limped, but the crutches were gone. In a way, the operation and the infection seemed like a distant dream.

"Man, you should have gotten up front in that picture," Thane said. "You made the winning catch!"

"Nah," Ty said. "I don't care. The only person I care about seeing me is you, and you saw it firsthand."

"What about your bodyguard, Agent Sutherland?" Thane asked. "He'd get a kick out of seeing you after carting you around for the tryouts and all that."

"You know," Ty said, "you're right. I forgot all about Agent Sutherland. He would like it. Oh, well."

The Bavaros appeared, and Thane talked excitedly to Mark Bavaro about the trip down to Miami, asking where the team would stay.

"There's a great new place called the Florida Grand," Bavaro said. "I got a block of rooms. It's not South Beach, but the place is five-star. It's not too far from the stadium and it's right on the edge of the Everglades. The Falcons are staying there."

"Two weeks till the Super Bowl? I'm surprised you got anything at all."

"The Giants' travel agent hooked me up," Bavaro said. "They had a corporate package that fell through. We'll be doing this thing in style."

Ty and Thane got into Thane's black Escalade and headed for home, both of them excited and grinning wide.

"You did awesome, Ty," Thane said as they pulled out onto the turnpike. "You made me proud."

Ty felt something grip his insides.

"What's the matter?" Thane glanced at him.

"Nothing."

"No, what?"

"Just what you said."

"About me being proud?" Thane said. "What's wrong with that?"

"Nothing." Ty turned his head away from Thane and wiped the corners of his eyes on the back of his hand. "It's just that's what he used to say. You sounded just like him."

"Who?" Thane asked.

"Dad."

CHAPTER THIRTY-ONE

MAYBE THE BEST PART about going to Miami for the week of the Super Bowl was missing school, the unexpected holiday, and the wistful look his Halpern teammates got in their eyes when they heard about him playing on a 7-on-7 team with Mark Bavaro's son.

Maybe the next best thing about the trip was being warm at the end of January. While New Jersey was wet and frozen, the air in Florida—even in the breezeway getting off the plane—was tropical. Thane rented a royal blue Mustang convertible. They put their luggage in the back and raced down the highway to the Florida Grand with the top down. The hotel looked like a white sand castle rising up out of a mangrove swamp. The driveway wound through a stand of ancient banyan trees, each with dozens of gray, narrow trunks growing into the same canopy of leaves. Bellmen in burgundy-colored uniforms with gold trim rushed down the stone steps to their car to take the luggage.

Their room looked out over the Everglades, an endless sea of green grass that switched and flowed in the wind with veins of glittering dark water. In the distance, little bumps of green suggested tree-covered islands that dotted the swamp. Directly below was a swimming pool with palm trees and a sandy beach that crept up to the edge of a broad body of dark water, which was part of a wide canal. The canal ran straight north and south and appeared to mark the eastern edge of the Everglades. The hotel also had a small marina jutting out into the dark water, where several fishing boats, skiffs, and WaveRunners were moored. On land, a rack of kayaks and canoes stood next to a thatched-roof hut.

Ty put his hands and nose on the window and stared.

"Want to go hit it?" Thane asked, tossing his bag onto a stand next to the dresser.

"The beach down there?"

"We can toss the ball around. Take a swim in the pool."

"Your knee."

Thane looked down at his leg and flexed it slowly. "I can throw passes, and I don't mean twenty laps, just a splash. I'm okay. They have me in the pool in therapy all the time anyway. I can do some self-rehab."

They spent the afternoon in the sun on the sand and

splashing in the pool. Ty kept his eyes open for signs of the Falcons players, but none appeared, and Thane told him the team was probably having a practice. After showers, they put on jeans and polo shirts and headed down the highway for South Beach. They pulled up to a fancy club right on the ocean. A young man in a white shirt and black pants parked the car, and Ty and Thane walked down a red carpet and into the crowd of people among white umbrellas and wide wood lounge chairs with thick white cushions. Music, laughter, and the hum of talking filled the air, along with smoke from several beach fires. Above, beyond the halo of light from the fires and city lights, the star-filled sky almost seemed to glow.

"And you get paid to just show up to this?" Ty asked.

Thane nodded. They checked in at a table and received bronze bracelets that would get them whatever food or drinks they wanted. Ty saw something go by on a tray, cherry red in a tall glass with a pink umbrella and a strawberry floating in the ice.

"That?" Ty asked.

Thane signaled to a waitress and asked for two of whatever they were without any alcohol. The two brothers found an empty lounge chair and sat down to watch the people move past, men and women elegantly dressed with brilliant gold watches, diamond necklaces, and sunglasses even though it was nighttime.

"We're kind of underdressed." Ty looked down at

what he had thought were pretty nice clothes.

Thane looked at Ty, then at his own clothes, and shrugged. "We're okay."

"Not like these people," Ty said.

Thane waved a hand in the air. "It doesn't matter what you look like on the outside. I mean, you don't want to be a disgrace or anything, but we've got nice clothes on. Not fancy, but nice. Respectable. People who judge you by what you wear or how good you look aren't worth knowing anyway."

Ty absorbed his older brother's words. And as he looked around, spotting other NFL star players—like Drew Brees, Troy Polamalu, and Adrian Peterson—his excitement grew.

Someone called his brother's name. Ty looked and saw Seth Cole, the New York Jets' owner. The owner reminded Ty of pictures he'd seen in history books of war prisoners, men with dark and empty eyes, even if they were smiling. Next to the owner stood Brett Favre. Ty's mouth fell open.

"Come on," Thane said, tugging Ty along with him.

The owner asked how Thane's knee was feeling, then introduced the NFL legend.

"I like your hands, man," Favre said.

"I like the way you throw the ball," Thane said. "This is my little brother, Ty. He's a receiver, too."

"Hey, Ty," Favre said. "You got those big hands like your brother."

Ty felt his heart swell with pride, but he couldn't talk, only nod.

"Tiger, you brought your brother?" the Jets' owner said with a blank face. "Very nice."

"He's here for that NFL Seven-on-Seven Tournament," Thane said. "He's playing for Mark Bavaro's team. They won the New Jersey qualifier. The finals are Sunday morning, but we'll see."

"Excellent," the Jets' owner said. "I've got a young man who's a guest of mine he should meet. He's here for the tournament, too. The team from Georgia."

The owner turned to a woman who stood behind him. She had long brown hair pulled into a ponytail. She wore no makeup but was pretty anyway, with her big green eyes and a bright smile. The owner said something to her. She turned back and ushered a girl Ty's age into the group. She had long dark hair and almond-shaped brown eyes. Her tan skin looked even darker because of the white summer dress she wore. Behind the girl was a boy in jeans and a polo shirt, just like Ty.

When Ty saw the boy's face, he recognized him instantly, and the shock of who he was made Ty stammer.

CHAPTER THIRTY-TWO

THE NFL OWNER BOWED to the young girl and the woman, then turned to Ty and Thanc. "This is Tessa White. She's here this week with our NFC champions. She's with the Falcons PR staff. And this lovely young spitfire—I use that as a term of affection—is Tate McGreer. Finally, a face you might recognize if you've been watching ESPN, or maybe you saw him on *Larry King* . . ."

"Troy White," Brett Favre said, extending his hand for a shake. "Hey, buddy, you ought to come to Minnesota next year. Don't listen to Mr. Cole here. I could use someone to tell me what defense the doggone Packers are gonna be in. You need to be wearing purple."

To his credit, Troy White blushed.

"The deal is already done, I'm afraid." The Jets' owner

put a hand on Brett Favre's shoulder and winked. "You may have the fastest release throwing the football, but I'm quicker with a checkbook. Troy, meet Tiger Lewis, and this is his brother, Ty. Sounds like you two might go at it this week in the Seven-on-Seven Tournament."

Ty held out his hand and shook Troy's iron grip.

Troy met his gaze with a steady eye. "Northern New Jersey, right? You're in the other bracket. We won't play you guys unless we both make it to the finals."

"No reason that can't happen," Ty said.

"I feel sorry for you if you do," Tate McGreer said to Ty.

"Why's that?" Ty asked.

Tate shrugged. "Anyone who plays against Troy won't stand a chance."

"You can't say that." Ty felt his face grow warm. "Mark Bavaro's son is our quarterback, and we've got a great team."

"I can say it." Tate spoke plainly, without anger or any kind of emotion. "'Cause it's true. That's all."

Ty didn't even know how to respond, but he was saved when the waitress appeared and delivered the red drinks Thane and Ty had ordered. Ty accepted his but felt a little silly when he saw the way Troy looked at the drink.

Tate said, "That's neat-looking. What is it?"

"Here, have some." Ty didn't know if it was because he was nervous, or flustered, or what, but the words came out of his mouth sounding cross, and he didn't mean them that way.

Even the sound of his words wouldn't have been a big deal if—at the same moment—the Jets' owner hadn't stepped sideways and onto Ty's foot. The heel of his shoe came down just so on the nail of Ty's big toe, sending a shock wave of pain up his leg. As a reflex, Ty yanked his foot free. The momentum tilted him off balance, and he lunged forward. The big red drink flew from his hand.

Everyone in the small group saw where the drink was headed, and everyone gasped.

CHAPTER THIRTY-THREE

TATE'S SHRIEK MADE HALF the nightclub stop and stare. Her dress looked like a horror movie, with red spattered all down its front and pink slush looking like bits of gore. Troy gripped Ty's arm and shoved him away.

"What's wrong with you?" Troy glared at Ty with clenched fists.

Ty could only swallow. Thane wore a look of surprise and didn't say a word.

"I . . . I didn't mean to," Ty said, but it sounded more angry than apologetic, even to Ty. He wanted to say that the owner had stepped on his foot, but Seth Cole's dark look scared him into silence.

Tate looked around at the gaping crowd and huffed. "Can you take me back to the hotel, Ms. White?"

"You don't have to go, Tate," Troy's mom said softly. "You can stay."

"I don't mind looking silly," Tate said, studying the mess. "But it's kind of sticky, if you don't mind."

"Of course." Troy's mom put her arm around Tate and led her off toward the entrance. Troy gave Ty one more hateful look before following the two of them.

"I'm sorry, Mr. Cole," Thane said to the Jets' owner.

The owner looked at Ty with eyes as lifeless as glass before narrowing them slightly and slipping off into the crowd.

"What the heck?" Thane said when they were alone.

"He stepped on my foot," Ty said.

"Who?"

"Mr. Cole. He stepped on my toe and I fell. I was offering her some, not throwing it at her."

Thane scowled at Ty. "What'd I tell you about what people say? Who cares if she said you can't beat him? I told you, that doesn't matter. You save it for the football field."

"I wasn't not saving anything! Why don't you believe me?" Ty turned and ran, through the crowd, past the fire pits, and out into the night on the empty beach. He turned so that the water was on his right and ran down the hard-packed surface where the waves still licked the sand. Above the thump of music from the party, Ty heard Thane calling his name.

The smell of dead sea animals rode the salty breeze. Ty stopped and turned and saw the outline of his brother's shape against the flickering lights of the party. Thane limped slightly as he made his way toward the water. Ty kept going down the beach, but he walked backward, watching to see what his brother would do. Ty just wanted some time alone. He figured his brother would tire of calling him and return to the party, but Thane fished the cell phone from his pocket and used it to light up the sand in front of him. Thane bent over to study the tracks in the firm sand, and presumably found Ty's because he started heading down the beach as well.

Instead of continuing on, Ty walked to the very edge of the waves, where his tracks would be washed away. He went another twenty yards, then ran and jumped up into the dry sand where no tracks could be found. He jogged all the way to the sea grass and sat down on the edge of a small dune. There was something exciting about outsmarting his brother and watching him move down the beach in the faint light from the stars without knowing that Ty was there. Thane would stop every few feet and check the footprints with his phone.

Just as Ty started to feel guilty about the trick, he caught the faraway movement of another dark shape, a man leaving the party and heading for the water without the help of any light or cell phone. Ty thought it was someone just taking a walk, but after a minute, he realized that when Thane stopped, the dark figure behind him stopped too. Ty blinked and rubbed his eyes, thinking that somehow the dark must be playing tricks on him. He watched for several more minutes.

When Thane turned around and the figure crouched down low on the sand so as not to be seen, Ty felt his heart race.

Thane was being followed, and not by a friend.

Ty didn't know what to do.

Ty could tell that Thane had no idea anyone was there. The figure moved suddenly closer. Thane bent over to study the sand, searching for tracks in the light of the cell phone.

Ty looked up and down the beach but saw no one to help.

"Thane!" Ty shouted. "Look out!"

Thane spun around and cried out in pain.

CHAPTER THIRTY-FOUR

TY'S HEART EXPLODED IN his chest. He dashed across the sand, stumbling and falling face-first, filling his mouth with the dry grains so that he spit and swiped at his face as he recovered and sprinted toward his fallen brother.

From the corner of his eye, Ty saw the figure racing back up the beach. In front of him, Thane lay still and silent.

Ty threw himself down on his knees beside his brother.

"Thane!" he cried. "Thane!"

Thane growled with pain, with eyes wide open and jaw clenched tight. Ty felt a wave of relief, even though tears continued to stream down his cheeks.

"I'm sorry," Ty said. "I'm so stupid. Are you okay? Thane?"

Thane gritted his teeth and sat up slowly, reaching for his knee. "I can't believe I spun around like that."

"He was following you." Ty's words came out in a flurry. "I thought he was going to get you. I had to yell."

Thane shook his head and felt the injured joint with both hands. "I don't know what I did to it, but it felt like it did when I tore it."

"You don't think you tore it again?" Ty asked.

"I don't know. They screwed the ligament into the bone, but they told me to be careful. Technically I should still be wearing a brace. Help me up."

Ty helped his brother struggle to his feet and allowed Thane to lean heavily on his shoulder. Slowly, they began to move up the beach. Thane used his bad leg carefully, putting very little weight on it and snatching up steps with his good leg.

"I thought you were dead," Ty said. The flickering flames from the party were like kaleidoscopes of orange and yellow light in his eyes.

"I'm okay," Thane said, but Ty could hear the agony in his voice.

"Who was that, Thane? Why would someone be following you?" Ty hoped there was another answer besides what he feared most: that the D'Amico mob had followed them down and were still looking for a chance at revenge.

"Maybe he wasn't," Thane said.

Ty shook his head violently. "That's what I wanted to think, but I swear, every time you stopped, he stopped, and when you looked back that one time, he ducked down in the sand so his shape wouldn't stand out against the lights."

"I felt like someone was watching me," Thane said, "but maybe he was . . . I don't know, looking for shells or something. Maybe he dropped his keys."

"But why run when you spun around?" Ty asked.

"Maybe you scared him," Thane said. "That must be it."

Ty didn't even want to say what he thought it was because it seemed that it might somehow make it true, but he couldn't help himself. "You don't think it was *them*, do you?"

Thane stopped hobbling. He took the back of Ty's neck and gently turned Ty's face to look into his eyes. "You've got to stop already. We're fine. It was someone looking for something who got scared when you yelled and I screamed. Man, that hurt like heck. I hope I didn't pull the screws out."

They walked around the outside edge of the party to where they could pick up their car. The valets looked sympathetically at Thane's expression of pain but said nothing as he and Ty climbed into the rented Mustang.

"You can drive okay?" Ty asked.

"I only need one leg for that."

Back at the hotel, Thane stripped off his jeans to reveal a knee that was swollen and red. The crimson and purple scars from his surgery puckered the skin around them from where the stitches had held the skin together tight.

"Can you get me a bag of ice?" Thane asked.

Ty scooted down the hallway and filled two plastic bags with ice from the machine. Thane packed the injured knee and lay back against the headboard of the bed, looking out over the Everglades.

Thane raised his bad leg. "I think it's going to be okay. When it was torn, I could feel it swinging loose. It's not doing that now. I probably just strained it."

Ty nodded, relieved. He brushed his teeth and got ready for bed before he returned to Thane's room. "I didn't spill that drink on purpose, Thane."

Thane lay with his eyes closed and his head back, and for a moment, Ty thought he might have fallen asleep.

"You better get to sleep," Thane said without opening his eyes. "Tomorrow is a big day for you guys. You didn't come down here to lose, did you?"

"No."

"Good, then get to sleep."

"I really didn't," Ty said.

Thane sighed. "I know. I believe you. Get to sleep."

Ty felt a flood of relief. He began to close the door, then stopped. "You think that Troy White is really what they say he is?"

"Mr. Cole isn't in the habit of paying people for things they can't do," Thane said without moving.

"Then how can we even hope to win this thing?"

Thane opened one eye, like a lizard looking for the source of some strange noise. "Let's just get to the finals, and if they get there too, we'll worry about it then. Okay? And, we're going to have to get in touch with that girl tomorrow and buy her a new dress."

"Okay, Thane." Ty felt a thrill go through him. He closed the door, then opened it again. "Thane? I love you."

"I love you, too, buddy. I always will. Spilled drink or no spilled drink. Knee or no knee."

When he got to his own room, Ty stood in the dark staring out at the glow of the night sky where it met the horizon beyond the endless Everglades. He couldn't say exactly why, but even though he had embarrassed himself and his brother tonight, he was eager to give the girl named Tate a new dress. In fact, the thought of seeing her again left a smile pasted on his face that wouldn't go away.

CHAPTER THIRTY-FIVE

ONLY THE CHAMPIONSHIP GAME of the 7-on-7 Tournament would be played at the Dolphins' stadium. The preliminary rounds were to take place at the University of Miami's football practice fields. The practice fields had surprisingly large bleachers, and they were full. With sixty-four teams from across the country, Ty wasn't surprised. He hopped down out of the shuttle bus Mark Bavaro had hired to transport them from the hotel to the games and scanned the crowd, looking for Thane. Then he sent a text, only to learn that his older brother hadn't arrived yet.

Thane texted him again.

GOOD LUCK!

Ty smiled and fell in line with his teammates as they wound their way through the crowd and out onto the field, led by their coach, Mark Bavaro. The North New Jersey Raptors wore deep red jerseys with white numbers. Their opponents would be the Kansas Storm, wearing powder blue with black numbers. The kids from Kansas didn't look that much bigger than the Raptors, but they did look fast. Ty couldn't keep from noticing as they warmed up how quick the hands of the cornerbacks were. They practiced a press coverage against their own teammates, and their hands shot out quick as frog tongues, connecting with the wide receivers like practiced boxers, and knocking them this way and that. By the time the receivers got free from these jams, they were too late to get to where they should be for the quarterback to throw the ball.

Ty bit his lip and warmed up with his own team. The Raptors defense played very little press coverage. Instead, they played more zone defense, where defenders would drop back to preassigned spots on the field—setting up a net of sorts—then reading the quarterback's eyes and the receivers' patterns to break up the pass or hopefully intercept the ball. Since the Raptors defense played zone, that was mostly what Ty had practiced against the past few weeks.

Ty liked playing against zone defenses, because he could use his brains to figure out the shape of the net and then his speed to get to the open holes that always existed. Press coverage was a bit different. When a team pressed, you had to be physical at the line of scrimmage, either slapping down their hands or plowing through the blows like a battleship. Ty's long thin arms and skinny frame weren't really built for either one of those things.

Mark Bavaro brought them together and urged them to give it their all.

"We win this one," the old player said, "and I've got a couple of tricks that'll get us all the way to the finals. This one is tough because we haven't seen these guys before, but if we get past them, there isn't going to be another team we play who we won't already have figured out. Trust me—I'll explain later—but we've got to win this one, guys."

They chanted "win" three times, then broke their huddle. The Raptors won the toss and got the ball first. Ty walked out onto the field with his offensive teammates, trying to keep his back straight and his head tall, hoping he looked more confident than he felt. He stepped into the huddle and glanced up into the stands for his brother, thinking he must be there by now. David Bavaro called the play, they broke the huddle, and Ty approached the line.

One of the Storm cornerbacks bounced into position in front of Ty, his rabbit-quick hands already flickering. One of the cornerback's teammates shouted at him. "Hey, Moby, try not to hurt that skinny kid!"

Ty ignored the remark and took one more quick look into the stands.

That's when he saw a face that made him freeze in terror.

CHAPTER THIRTY-SIX

BEYOND HIS COUSIN CHARLOTTE'S strange behavior and unpredictable mood swings, Ty hadn't given much thought at all to girls. It wasn't that he didn't like girls, it was just that he didn't think about them. His mind was on sports and books and doing well in school. Girls filled up the same space in the hallways and classrooms as boys did. The only difference he ever really noticed about girls was that they had their own sports teams.

The girl named Tate had changed that.

She scared him and made him dizzy with excitement all at the same time.

Spilling his drink on her the night before had been a moment so horrible that he was sure he'd never forget it. But, spilling the drink also made it possible for him to see her again. They *had* to get her a new dress.

His brother said so. Ty already imagined several noble ways they might present Tate with her new dress: over dinner in a fancy restaurant, out on a grand yacht they might charter for an afternoon on the ocean, or beside a campfire on the beach with the darkness closing in.

What he hadn't considered was seeing Tate at the football field. Worse would be Tate seeing him, especially when he was about to get battered around like a punching bag. Ty averted his eyes and settled into his stance as the quarterback began his cadence. He tried not to notice the burning intensity in the cornerback named Moby's eyes, but they drew his attention like a pinball is drawn to a magnet. The bright yellow eyes swirled like a madman's, and Moby made little huffing noises like a dog's frantic sniffing.

The ball was snapped.

Ty took off.

Moby hit him square in the chest, and Ty's feet left the earth.

CHAPTER THIRTY-SEVEN

BAVARO THREW AN INCOMPLETE pass downfield to one of the receivers who was able to get off the line of scrimmage. The whistle blew, and Ty's eyes went toward Tate's seat in the stands.

She looked at him with real concern, then smiled uncertainly and waved.

Ty blushed and gave a little wave back as he got to his feet. He dusted the grass off the sleeve of his shirt and realized that Tate hadn't been looking at him at all. She broke out into a full grin now as Troy White and his mom walked up the bleachers' steps and gave her hugs before sitting down beside her. Troy wore a dark blue jersey with white numbers, and Ty figured he must be playing soon. Ty only hoped that the boy from Georgia—because he was finding his seat—hadn't seen Ty get knocked off his feet.

"What happened?" David Bavaro asked Ty in the huddle.

"He pressed me."

"They rolled their safety to the other side of the field. You should have been wide open," the quarterback said. "Come on, Ty. You gotta get past the press."

"He's pretty good." Ty spoke in a mutter. "I'll try."

Bavaro called the play, and they broke the huddle. Ty jogged to the line, hoping that this time another Kansas player might be covering him. He glanced up into the stands and saw Tate sitting with the Whites. Troy stared right at him, and Ty pretended not to notice.

The same cornerback, Moby, bounced toward Ty and hunkered down across the line from him. Ty gritted his teeth and exhaled. He just had no luck.

Ty got into his stance, hands up, feet staggered, eyes straight ahead, looking through the bouncing, snarling, fist-flickering cornerback.

David Bavaro began his cadence, and Ty glanced to the inside to see how much space he'd have to run. The ball was snapped. Ty gave a head fake to the outside, then burst back toward the inside. Moby didn't miss a beat. He never went for the head fake at all, but instead shot both hands out into Ty's chest. Ty staggered sideways, and Moby jammed him again, sending Ty toward the middle of the field and completely out of the pattern.

When Bavaro threw to the crossing route over the

middle, Moby leaped up and tipped the ball. The ball sailed, end over end, like a kickoff. One of the Kansas safeties jumped up and snatched it, accelerating past Ty, dodging Bavaro, and scoring a defensive touchdown for the Storm.

Ty looked haplessly at Bavaro. The quarterback could only shake his head, turn away, and walk off the field. Ty hung his own head and followed at a jog. When he got to the sideline, Mark Bavaro stood waiting for him, banging the side of his leg with a clipboard. Bavaro's face looked like it was ready to explode.

"Ty," the coach said, pointing toward the bench, "have a seat."

CHAPTER THIRTY-EIGHT

IN CASE TATE WAS watching, Ty didn't go straight to the bench because he didn't want her to see that happen. Ty wandered over to the Gatorade table and sipped at a cup. He got an idea and headed for Larry Oppenheimer, one of the dads, who was a professional trainer and helping out with the team.

"Mr. Oppenheimer," Ty said, making his face long, "could you take a look at my tape? I think it's too tight."

Mr. Oppenheimer looked at him impatiently because his son was playing linebacker on defense right next to Michael Strahan Jr. and he obviously wanted to watch the game.

"Here, hop up here." The trainer walked over and patted the bench.

Ty hopped up and watched with intense concern as

the trainer stripped off his shoe and sock and examined the tape.

"It looks fine. Your foot's not red or anything, Ty." The trainer glanced over his shoulder at the action. "You want me to retape it?"

"No, thanks, Mr. Oppenheimer. I just wanted to make sure I wasn't cutting off the circulation. I'll work through it."

The trainer gave Ty a sympathetic look before moving back toward the sideline. Ty felt a weight in his gut over tricking the trainer, but he preferred that feeling to having Tate and Troy White witness his benching. As it was, they might think he was hurt, and that's why he wouldn't be returning to the field. Ty sat there with his ankle still up on the bench, as if he really was hurt.

The problem for Ty was that the longer he sat there faking it, the worse he felt. When he heard Thane's voice from behind him and saw his brother leaning over the fence separating the stands from the bench area, Ty put his leg down and stood up.

"What are you doing?" Thane asked. "What's with your ankle?"

"Oh, my tape was a little tight. That's all." Ty knew his face must be red as a fire engine.

"That's no reason to sit there on the bench. What happened? Why aren't you out there?"

Ty glanced at Coach Bavaro, who was shouting something to his son as they drove down the field, the

Raptors now back on offense.

"I had trouble getting off the jam." Ty looked at his cleats.

"Bavaro benched you?"

"It happened twice. I messed up. The guy covering me jammed me all the way into the middle, then jumped up and tipped the ball. They picked it off and scored."

Thane pressed his lips tight enough so that his mouth was nothing but a paper cut in the bottom of his face. A warm breeze wafted Thane's brown hair across his forehead until he swept it away.

"Well," Thane finally said, "it is what it is. Just be ready if you get another chance. What did you do with your eyes?"

"My eyes?" Ty said.

"Did you look where you were going?"

Ty thought for a moment. "I did."

"Okay, that happens," Thane said. "Just remember, if you get the chance, *don't* look where you're going to go. Eyes straight ahead, no matter what. Then, give him a double move. He'll jam on the second move, and you'll be gone. Got it?"

"Got it."

Ty walked back into the mix of teammates standing behind their coaches on the sideline. He studied the cornerback Moby. Moby shut down every Raptors receiver he went up against. Coach Bavaro sent two different players in at Ty's position, but neither of them could get free. The game progressed with each team trading scores, keeping it close.

Ty took a deep breath and tapped Coach Bavaro on the shoulder. "Coach, I think I can get past that guy. My brother gave me an idea."

"Your brother?" Bavaro looked around, saw Thane standing by the fence, and gave him a nod. "We'll see."

Bavaro turned his attention back to the field.

As the clock wound down into the final few minutes, Coach Bavaro glanced Ty's way, and Ty began to think that he just might get that other chance.

CHAPTER THIRTY-NINE

THE RAPTORS WERE DOWN by two points.

Only twenty-two seconds remained in the game.

When the coach called Ty's name, he ran out onto the field without taking even a peek at where Tate sat with her friend Troy White. Ty didn't care. He was zeroed in on Moby, and on beating him good.

"We got to go deep." David Bavaro stared at his four receivers without blinking. "Double ninety-seven strong seam. One of you guys has got to get open. On two, ready . . .

"Break!"

Ty jogged out to the edge of the field and lined up on the forty-five-yard line, going into the end zone. From the corner of his eye, he saw Moby approaching him, bouncing on his toes, hands jittery. Ty set up in his stance, coiling his muscles, and stared straight ahead.

He ignored Moby's huffing sounds and refused to let his eyes wander. David Bavaro began the cadence.

Moby's bouncing increased and he began to mutter. "Gonna jam you. Gonna jam you good."

Ty didn't react, but on the snap of the ball, he gave a head fake outside, then back inside. Moby's hands shot out and struck Ty, but Ty had already turned sideways and started back to the outside: the double fake. Moby's blow glanced off Ty's ribs, and Ty shot past the cornerback, racing straight down the sideline.

As he ran, Ty sensed Moby on his heels. Ty had beaten the jam, but the lightning-quick cornerback had recovered faster than Ty had imagined. Ty kept his cool and pumped his arms, smooth and fast, like pistons in an engine. At twenty yards, Ty turned his head—just a bit—to see if the ball had been thrown his way.

It had.

The ball had already reached the peak of its arc and it fell now on a trajectory that would actually fall short of where Ty would be if he kept running at full speed.

Ty felt sick. In that same split second, he knew that if he slowed to catch the ball, Moby would catch him. It was the only way, though. Ty slowed, turned, and leaped up into the air for the ball. Moby caught him and spun on one foot like a dancer, leaping high, higher than Ty, and snatching the ball from the air before Ty could even touch it.

CHAPTER FORTY

THE JETS WERE PLAYING the Patriots in New York in late December. It was the last game of the regular season. The Jets needed to win if they were to make the playoffs. Only seconds remained in that game as well when the ball was thrown up to Tiger Lewis. When the ball came up short, Patriots cornerback Leigh Bodden jumped up in front of Tiger and grabbed what looked like a game-ending interception.

That was not what happened, though. Instead of giving up, Ty's brother swatted at the ball in the cornerback's hands, spilling it from his grip and causing the pass to fall incomplete to the turf. Two plays later, Tiger outmaneuvered the Patriots secondary in the end zone to pull in the winning catch and send the Jets into the playoffs. Tiger was ESPN's Player of the Week.

When Ty asked his older brother about the play with Bodden, Thane bent at the waist, lowering his face so that it was even with Ty's. "The only statistic that matters is wins and losses. Never forget that. No one gives you credit for breaking up an interception, not like they do when you catch a touchdown pass, but breaking up an interception is every bit as important as scoring a touchdown. When that cornerback gets his hands on the ball? Remember this: It's your ball. It belongs to you. You go get that thing like some punk stole your lunch money. You hear me?"

Ty nodded ferociously. He felt embarrassed at the way people stared at them. They were talking in the players' parking lot after the game. Everyone else was celebrating cheerfully, and the intensity of Thane's voice was like nails on a chalkboard.

The impression stayed with Ty. He knew because when Moby's fingers wrapped themselves around the point of the ball, Ty felt an outrage his brother would be proud of. It was the outrage of watching someone steal from you. Even as they both fell back to the ground, Ty made a fist and punched up under Moby's arm.

The ball popped free, toppling up end over end, sailing past Ty's head and falling to the turf. Ty landed in a heap with Moby on top of him. Moby cursed and jumped up, dusting himself off as he walked away without even a glance at Ty. Ty climbed to his feet and jogged back to the cluster of teammates waiting for the play to be called.

David Bavaro met Ty outside the huddle, slapped him on the shoulder, and said, "I owe you big for that. We all do. Heck of a play, Ty."

Ty grinned.

"Can you beat him like that again? I won't come up short this time. That was on me. You had him."

"Yeah," Ty said, sounding more confident than he felt, "I can beat him."

"Good." The quarterback slapped Ty's back again. "Let's do it."

They got into the huddle, and David Bavaro called the play.

"The same play?" someone asked. "Who runs the same play twice?"

"Exactly," David Bavaro said. "No one. Except we will, and they'll hesitate, thinking we wouldn't do that, and one of you is going to get open and we're going to win this thing."

They broke the huddle. Ty jogged to the line. Moby set up in front of him and began slapping his own head and chattering to himself like a crazy man.

"Jam you down. Jam you down good! No one beats Moby!"

Ty's mind swirled. Thane had told him how to beat Moby once, but he hadn't explained how to do it again. Could he do the same thing he did before? Moby would expect that, right? Ty thought he should probably fake inside, then out, then go back in, reversing what he'd done before. Then he thought he should just fake one way, but what about a triple fake? That wouldn't work, because it would take too long.

Ty kept his eyes ahead while he thought. Before he could decide, the ball was snapped. Ty automatically did exactly what he'd done the previous play, faking outside, then in, then darting back out. The jam never came. Moby retreated instead, opting to play it safe and match speed with speed. Ty took off, closing the three-yard gap between him and Moby, but knowing instinctively that he'd never outrun the crazy cornerback after that kind of head start.

But in that same fraction of a second, Ty had an idea.

He remembered another thing he'd learned from his brother.

CHAPTER FORTY-ONE

TY HAD GROWN UP worshipping his older brother, Thane. With ten years between them, most people were surprised at how close the two of them were. Even before the death of their parents, Thane always made time for Ty and shared with him the things he'd learned as an elite athlete. Many times, Thane would tell Ty stories about things that had happened, and Ty soaked up every word.

One bit of advice Thane gave him didn't come wrapped in a story, but Thane said it with the conviction of Moses reciting the Ten Commandments.

"You don't ever quit." Thane had spoken these words one day after the two of them watched a football game on TV. "That's the rule. You never give up. You want to be a champion, you have to think that way, in everything you do. You never stop. You let yourself start to think that way, then the one time you could pull out a win because

of some freak luck, you're not ready for it. Maybe it's only once in a lifetime, but that's one win you'd never have, and who knows what that one win could do."

This had worked for Ty before and he knew better than to slow down for even an instant, whatever the situation looked like. There were a number of things that could happen: The cornerback could trip, he could misread the throw, he could get a cramp in his leg or pull a hamstring. All unlikely, but Ty wanted to be a champion. He wanted to be like Thane, so he ran.

When the ball went into the air, Ty knew it hadn't been thrown to him. Moby broke off from his coverage of Ty, either to make a play on the ball, or tag the receiver if he caught it and the other defender missed. The slot receiver to Ty's inside had run a corner route underneath Ty's straight run up the field. Bavaro threw to the shorter route, knowing they still would have time for another play or two if it was caught.

It wasn't caught.

Instead, the defender covering the underneath route tipped the ball, redirecting it. Over Moby's head it went. The crazy cornerback threw a hand up, desperate but quick, nicking it in midair without slowing it down much.

Ty spun on one leg, opening his hips and reaching wide with his left hand, extending it fully from his body as he spun.

Thunk.

The ball landed in his hand. Ty held on and kept

spinning, landing on his other leg and continuing on down the field and into the end zone.

Touchdown.

Ty's teammates rushed him, jumping and leaping and screaming at the tops of their lungs. Even the old NFL star Mark Bavaro ran out and flung Ty into the air. Ty laughed and held the ball up high. A one-handed miracle catch. The kind of thing that made you a champion.

When Ty looked up into the stands this time, he was eager to see the faces of the kids from Georgia. What he saw disappointed him. Instead of staring down at him from their seats, Tate, Troy, and Troy's mom were nearly at the bottom of the bleachers' steps, paying no attention at all to the drama in the end zone.

Ty ignored it and tried his best to enjoy the thrill of the celebration. He watched with clenched teeth as the Raptors defense held off the Kansas team for two more offensive plays. The gun sounded, and the Raptors lined up to shake hands. Afterward, Mark Bavaro gathered up his team.

"Outstanding job by a lot of you guys," the coach said. "Ty, nice comeback by you, my friend. That's what this game is about, guys. It looked like Ty was shut down for good, but everyone struggled against that kid, and Ty stayed ready and when he got a second chance, he delivered. That's football. You gotta be ready to come back. No one ever goes through this game as a front-runner. It just doesn't happen. It's a game of comebacks, and a game of character. Ty showed us all about character."

Ty blushed and looked down, enjoying the praise. Coach Bavaro told them all to relax and enjoy the rest of the day.

"We'll get together after dinner tonight," the coach said. "I've got a meeting room for seven thirty, Salon G on the third floor. I'll have film on whoever we're going to play next, and your coaches and I will have a game plan ready to go. I told you the first game would be our toughest early on because we didn't know what we were up against. We had no film on them.

"You'll see how this works when I show you the film tonight. No one is going to outcoach us in this thing. We'll break down the film we've got on our next opponent like it's an NFL game. We'll know what coverage they like to run in certain situations and we'll know what plays they'll run against our defense. It'll give us a huge advantage. You'll see."

They gave a chant to win and broke the gathering. Ty found Thane and hugged him tight.

"You did it," Thane said.

"*You* helped. Coach Bavaro said he and the other coaches are going to scout the teams we'll be playing next. Do you want to watch a couple games with me?"

"Nothing to do but sit in the sun," Thane said. "Sure. Let's see some of the competition."

Ty didn't tell his brother that what he really wanted to see was Troy White and, more importantly, maybe sitting in the stands, his friend Tate McGreer.

CHAPTER FORTY-TWO

TY LOOKED AROUND FOR the dark blue jerseys worn by the Georgia team. Two fields over, he saw them.

"Come on," Ty said. "Over here. I want to watch that Georgia team."

"You won't play them until the finals," Thane said. "That's if you both get there."

"Gotta think positive." Ty tugged his brother's arm.

As they approached the bleachers, the ball went flying through the air. Ty's eyes followed the ball as it sailed past the defenders, landing perfectly in the open arms of a sprinting Georgia wide receiver. Half the crowd cheered. Troy White jumped into the air with his teammates.

Ty saw Tate now, standing up to clap along with the other Georgia fans. Next to her was Troy's mom.

"This way." Ty led Thane up the bleacher steps

without hurrying since Thane was still moving slow with his bad knee.

"Hello, Ms. White." Ty nodded at the mom before extending a hand to Tate. "Hi, Tate. I wanted to apologize about last night."

Tate looked at him suspiciously.

"I really didn't mean to spill that drink on you," Ty said. "I was nervous is all, and it sounded different than I meant it. I wouldn't do something like that to someone, even if I was mad, which I really wasn't. I offered you some because it sounded like you wanted to try it. When I went to give it to you, Mr. Cole stepped right on my big toe and I jerked away and . . . I . . . that's how I spilled everything. I'm really sorry."

Tate looked at Troy's mom, and the two of them seemed to communicate without words. Finally, Ms. White smiled and Tate's face relaxed.

"That's okay," she said, taking Ty's extended hand. "Do you want to sit with us?"

"That would be great," Ty said, sitting down on the bench where they made room for him and Thane.

"Anyone tell you that you and Troy kind of look alike?" Tate asked.

Ty blushed and shook his head. "This one guy I know said that a couple weeks ago when we saw Troy on ESPN."

"Yeah, you kinda do," Tate said, staring for a second before ending the conversation by turning her attention back to the field.

"Hi," Thane said, holding out a hand to Troy's mom. "Tessa, right?"

"Yes," Ms. White said. "Is something wrong with your leg?"

"I had this knee rebuilt, and it flared up on me a little. Nice pass by your boy."

"Thank you."

"Ty, you had a great catch in your game," Tate said, leaning forward so she could talk around Tessa White.

Ty felt his face go warm. "We're going to buy you a new dress. If that's okay?"

Ty watched Ms. White give Tate a look. Tate seemed like she wanted to say yes, but was waiting for clearance from the Falcons PR woman. Finally, Ms. White nodded and Tate grinned.

"It was only Banana Republic," Tate said.

"I love Banana Republic," Ty said.

"We can go after this game," Thane said. "Stop by the Lincoln Road mall, get Tate a new dress, maybe even some lunch."

"That would be nice. I've heard about Lincoln Road," Ms. White said, directing her attention back to the field.

"Who knows," Thane said, "maybe we'll be neighbors up north, when you move."

"Maybe," Ms. White said. "Do you like New Jersey?"

"It's really nice," Thane said. "I'm from upstate New

York, though, so I'm used to the cold."

Tessa White shivered at just the thought. "Well, Mr. Cole made us an offer we couldn't refuse. I'm hoping we can find something where it's a bit on the quiet side."

"I'm telling you," Thane said, "there are plenty of places off Route Seventy-eight where you think you're a million miles away from the city and all the crowds. We're in Summit."

"That sounds nice." Tessa gave Thane a smile before returning her attention to the game.

They sat and watched together. Ty felt strange cheering for someone he hoped he'd beat if he got the chance, but it only made sense since they were sitting with Troy's mom and Tate, who yelled her head off.

Ty had to admit to himself that he felt a little jealous of the way Troy directed the offense and the defense of his team. On defense, Troy played free safety and made all the calls from the middle of the field, pointing and shouting and moving his teammates around like pieces on a chess board. Ty's rival had an uncanny knack for being wherever the ball was, so much so that Ty began to rethink his disbelief in the Georgia boy's mental abilities. By the time the game ended (with Troy's team winning by five touchdowns), Ty understood the simple certainty that Tate had when it came to Troy's team winning the whole tournament. He hated to admit it, but Ty had a hard time seeing how his team could compete.

"There's always luck," Tate said, as if she'd been reading Ty's mind.

"What?" Ty blinked at her.

"Luck is a big part of football," Tate said. "More than people think. Someone could get lucky and knock them out. Otherwise, as you can see, these guys look unbeatable."

"How do you know so much about football?" Ty asked.

"Me?" Tate pointed to her own chest. "I *play* football. Well, I'm a kicker. Really, I'm probably gonna end up a soccer player, but how many girls do you know who actually wear shoulder pads and a helmet?"

"None, I guess," Ty said.

"And I even make tackles on the kickoff." Tate smiled big. "I love football. That's how I met Troy and Nathan. He's our other best friend, but he's a lineman, and linemen don't play in Seven-on-Seven. Troy's mom invited him, too, but his aunt is getting married in San Diego. You should have seen Nathan's face, he almost busted an artery. We all played on the Duluth Tigers and we won the Georgia Junior Football League State Championship."

"That's great," Ty said, wanting to tell her about his own team's county championship, but it sounded weak next to a state championship.

"Yeah, and my dad's a huge Chicago Bears fan," Tate said. "You don't go in my house on Sunday wearing anything but their team colors, orange and midnight blue. I think my dad wishes I was a boy, but that's okay. My mom says he'll be glad when he's old. She says girls always take care of their parents better than boys when they're old."

Tate blushed. "I'm talking too much, but at least you know I'm not some ditz when I say they're gonna win this thing."

"They're good, but you never know." The competitor in Ty wasn't going to let him concede victory before the game had even been played, no matter how good the other team looked.

Together, they left the stands and met Troy to congratulate him. He was obviously surprised to see Ty and Thane and he didn't hide his displeasure. But when Tate explained how Ty had apologized, Troy seemed to soften and he thanked them for their praises.

"I saw that catch you made, too," Troy said to Ty. "You've got some serious speed."

"Who knows," Thane said. "Your mom might like it where we live in New Jersey. Maybe you two will end up at the same school."

"You never know where we'll live," Troy's mom said. "We'll all be Jets fans, though. That we do know."

"So, how about that trip to the mall?" Thane asked. "We can replace Tate's dress and maybe have lunch."

Troy's mom checked her watch. "I guess we could swing by. I don't know about lunch. The Falcons practice at three, and I've got some work to do beforehand."

"Just something quick," Thane said. "Only if you have time."

Troy's mom looked at Ty's brother for a moment, then said, "Tiger, I don't mean to embarrass you or anyone, but there's something you need to know."

CHAPTER FORTY-THREE

"I HAVE A VERY serious boyfriend," Troy's mom said.

Ty looked at his brother as Thane's face turned red.

"I didn't mean it like that," Thane said. "It's not that I wouldn't mean it like that. Wait, that came out wrong. Look, we just want to get Tate a new dress. We both feel bad about last night."

Ty nodded.

"And, as far as New Jersey"—Thane held his hands up in the air—"I'm just trying to be nice. I know Troy will be working with the team, so we're all on the same side. Or, we will be after the Super Bowl."

Troy's mom broke out into a smile and it was her turn to blush. "I didn't think . . . well, I wasn't sure. I just like to be up-front."

"And me too," Thane said. "So, let's go get Tate's

dress, and if we have time for something to eat, we'll do it. If not, another time. With your boyfriend, if you like."

"He's Seth Halloway," Troy said with obvious pride. "Her boyfriend."

"He's a great player," Thane said. "I watched him growing up."

Thane's words seemed to put everyone at ease. Ty and Thane got into their Mustang. Troy, his mom, and Tate followed them in a small four-door rental car of their own. They parked in a garage at one end of Lincoln Road mall and strolled down the open promenade to Banana Republic.

Inside, Tate said, "I got it from the sale rack."

Ty liked the way she didn't seem to mind buying something from the sale rack and he followed her there while Troy's mom asked him to try on a shirt. Troy gave Ty a look that seemed to be a warning before he disappeared with his mom.

"Here it is." Tate dug through a rack and pulled out a white dress. "But not in my size."

"What about one of those?" Thane said, pointing to a mannequin display of a much more elaborate white summer dress with colorful and delicate embroidery around the collar and hem.

"Well, that's beautiful," Tate said, "but my dress didn't cost that much."

Thane waved a hand in the air. "But we can't replace

it if they don't have your size, so we should get something at least as nice."

Troy's mom walked up to them and Thane explained the situation. Troy's mom thought for a moment, then said, "I think it's okay, Tate. Go ahead."

Tate grinned. A salesgirl got a dress off the rack for her to try, and Tate came out a few minutes later, looking fantastic.

"Done," Thane said, winking at Ty.

When they walked out, Troy's mom pointed at a place down the street. "Bella Cuba. I heard about that."

"Then you have time for lunch?" Thane asked.

They did, and the five of them sat down at a round table by the window for salads and sandwiches. Ty continued to be surprised at how much knowledge Tate had about football, and that was what the three kids talked about while Thane and Troy's mom talked about politics and art museums and some other uninteresting subjects.

Without warning, Troy's face went blank. His mouth hung open as he stared out the window behind Ty. Ty spun around, expecting something horrible but only seeing a steady stream of shoppers going by.

By the time Ty looked back around, Troy was already out of his chair and sprinting through the restaurant for the door.

"Troy?" Troy's mom shouted. "What's wrong?"

Troy didn't answer. He flung open the door, nearly

knocking over an older couple. The last thing Ty saw was Troy in a full sprint, flashing past the window, and disappearing into the crowd.

Ty looked at Tate. "What happened?"

Tate clenched her napkin and gave Troy's mom a fearful look.

CHAPTER FORTY-FOUR

"I'M SORRY," TROY'S MOM said to Thane. She wiped her mouth and laid her napkin down on the table before getting up and shouldering her purse. "Troy's been out of sorts lately. He does this sometimes. It's nothing to do with either of you, I promise. Tate, you finish your food. I'll go look for him. I'm sure I'll be back in a few minutes."

"I should go with you." Tate began to rise.

"No." Troy's mom raised a hand. "Please, Tate. Let me go alone."

They watched Troy's mom leave the restaurant and walk past the window, heading in the same direction as Troy. Tate hung her head and poked at a tomato wedge with her fork.

Thane cleared his throat and excused himself to use the bathroom.

They sat silently with the tinkle of silverware and the warm chatter of happy customers all around them.

"Can I help?" Ty asked.

Tate shook her head, and Ty didn't think she was going to say a word. He sipped his soda and looked out the window, surprised when she did finally speak.

"He thinks he sees his dad," Tate said.

"His dad?"

"It's a long story. His parents aren't together. He doesn't like to talk about it, so please don't say anything, okay? I just don't want you to think he's weird, because he's not."

"Okay, I won't." Ty felt a pang of jealousy. He wondered what it would be like to have a girl like Tate defend him for his strange behavior. She obviously cared a great deal for Troy.

"His parents . . . well, it's really bad between them. I think it's even possible Troy's dad does really show up places. I mean—"

Thane walked up and sat down, and Tate spoke no more. The check came, and Thane paid it after asking Tate if she'd like dessert. Just as Thane finished signing the credit card slip, Troy and his mom appeared in the window. Troy kept his eyes down, but his mom waved to them to come out.

When they stood in a small cluster outside the restaurant, Troy's mom said, "Sorry; Troy saw someone he thought he knew."

Troy's mom sounded cheerful, but Ty noticed the

lines of worry in her face. Tate put a hand on Troy's shoulder, but Troy didn't react. Ty could only wish he was Troy.

"That's fine." Thane sounded just as cheerful. "We were just glad to be able to get Tate her dress and have a little lunch."

"We were almost finished anyway, right?" Troy's mom sounded hopeful.

"Of course," Thane said.

Still cheerful, Troy's mom said, "The Falcons are having a sponsor party at the Florida Grand by the pool. You two are welcome to be our guests if you like."

"We're staying at the Florida Grand," Ty said, hopeful for another chance to see Tate.

"Great, then you'll join us?" Troy's mom said. "I'd love to have you meet Seth."

"Ty's got film study with his team, but we can meet you after that if there's time," Thane said.

In the car on the way back to the hotel, Ty said, "Tate told me Troy sometimes thinks he sees his dad. I guess it's pretty bad between his dad and mom."

Thane kept his eyes on the road. "That happens."

"It was still kind of weird," Ty said.

Thane shrugged. "I'm guessing that genius thing he's got makes living a normal life tough sometimes."

"What do you mean?"

"Well, sometimes people who are that smart can be a little odd. It's nothing bad, just that they see things in a different way. You've got to take the good with the bad, just like everything else."

"You think that's why he sees things?" Ty asked.

"Maybe."

Ty thought about that all the way back to the hotel. As they walked through the lobby, Ty was ready for a distraction, and he got it when he noticed a small poster board set up on an easel. The easel rested next to a towering white column and it looked like an advertisement for a movie.

MAN-EATERS!

Beneath the word were pictures of giant alligators thrashing the water with gaping tooth-filled jaws. Ty looked closer and tugged at Thane's arm.

"Can we do that?" Ty stabbed a finger toward the sign.

Thane looked at the poster board. "Man-eaters? Sure. Sounds fun."

CHAPTER FORTY-FIVE

THEY WERE TOLD TO dress in long sleeves and pants and to wear hats that could be sprayed with insect repellent to keep away the bugs. So Ty felt a little funny walking through the pool area dressed for a safari with everyone lounged out in sunglasses and bathing suits. When he saw Tate, he stopped short and nudged Thane.

"Can we ask Tate if she wants to come?"

"Sure," Thane said. "You ask her, and I'll meet you over there at the marina."

Ty opened his mouth to suggest that Thane be the one to invite her, but his older brother was already on the move, hobbling through the crowded pool area. When he'd blurted out the suggestion to Thane, Ty hadn't considered that he'd have to be the one to do the inviting. Ty looked around for signs of Troy White and his mom but saw none. He presumed Troy had gone to the Falcons practice with his mom.

Jittery with nerves, Ty swallowed and approached Tate. She lay back in a deck chair with her eyes hidden behind a pair of sunglasses. She wore a yellow bathing suit and her mouth wore the hint of a smile. In the chair next to Tate sat a middle-aged woman reading a book. The woman had stacked her hair high up on her head, and her sunglasses frames appeared to be made out of gold. Ty ignored her and stepped up to Tate.

Ty cleared his throat. "Um, do you want to see some alligators with us?"

Tate didn't move.

Ty looked around, his already sweaty face getting hotter.

"Um, we won't be gone long. There's supposedly some fifteen-footers out there."

Tate didn't speak.

"Well, I didn't mean to bug you," Ty said. "I just thought—"

Tate yawned without making another sound.

Ty sighed and turned to go.

"She can't hear you."

Ty spun around to see the woman with the fancy sunglasses looking at him over her book.

"Excuse me?"

"She can't hear you." The woman inclined her head toward Tate. "She's listening to an iPod."

Ty looked closer. He studied the long hair framing Tate's tan face and discovered just a hint of two white wires sticking from her ears. In the beach bag next to her chair, he saw the corner of an iPod peeking out at him.

"Oh," Ty said. "Thank you."

He stepped closer and nudged Tate's foot. She jumped and whipped off her sunglasses.

"What?" Tate glowered at him. "What are you doing?"

CHAPTER FORTY-SIX

"I'M SORRY." TY LOOKED at the woman, who ducked back behind her book, then back at Tate. "I just, I didn't know you were listening to music. I mean, I did know. I just asked you if you wanted to see some man-eaters and you didn't say anything and I was walking away and this lady told me you didn't hear me."

They both looked at the lady. She sat behind her book without any indication she had heard or said a thing.

"You scared me." Tate eyed him suspiciously. "What man-eaters?"

"Gators," Ty said, pointing toward the Everglades. "I saw a poster in the lobby. Fifteen-foot gators. They take you out in boats to see them. Thane and I are going. He said I could invite you. Do you want to go?"

Tate seemed to think about it. She picked her phone

out of the beach bag and dialed Troy's mom, asking permission. Tate nodded her head, then she smiled at Ty. "Will we be back by dinner?"

"Sure," Ty said.

"Did they really eat anyone?"

"I'm not sure," Ty said. "I read one time about a gator they cut open who ate a dog."

"A little one?"

"No, a chocolate Lab."

"Do I need to put something different on?" Tate pulled a beach shirt on over her bathing suit and tucked away her iPod earphones. She was obviously excited.

"Some pants and a hat," Ty said. "For the bugs. But we can wait for you. Is Troy around? Do you want to ask him?"

"He's at practice, but thanks. Do you go right from the marina?"

"Yes," Ty said.

"Meet you there in ten." Tate hurried off toward the hotel.

Ty didn't feel the ground beneath his feet, but somehow he made it over to the marina, where Thane already sat in the bow of a long skiff, lying back with his hands behind his head, catching some sun on his face. In the back of the boat a young man stood with drooping shoulders. A messy black thatch of hair hung down, nearly covering his cloudy gray eyes and the metal ball pierced through his bird-beak nose. The ink-black hair

made his pale white skin seem whiter than milk. His
scrawny legs were only outdone by matchstick arms
tracked by green veins. A faded black T-shirt said:
"Girls Love Pale Skinny Guys."

Thane sat up. "Ty, meet Gumbo. Gumbo, my little
brother, Ty."

Ty waved, and the slouched-over young man showed
off his buck teeth in what might have been a wince or
a smile.

"Gumbo?" Ty whispered to Thane as he sat down in
front. "Not much of a tour guide for a fancy place like
this."

"He grew up in these swamps." Thane spoke out
loud, as if Ty hadn't whispered, and Ty scowled at his
brother. "Your girlfriend joining us?"

Ty blushed. "She's not my girlfriend."

Thane punched his shoulder. "You know I'm kidding."

Gumbo picked his nose and looked up at the sky.
"Gonna rain, but not 'fore we see some man-eaters.
That much, I promise."

Ty didn't see a cloud in sight and figured the guy
was off his rocker. Tate arrived wearing jeans, a long-
sleeved T-shirt, and a white Falcons hat. Gumbo fired
up the outboard motor and, standing in the back of the
boat, used a long steering rod to maneuver the boat out
into the main channel. They took a right and wound
through a small creek until they came to yet another

channel. Gumbo went left this time, then took a second right into another snaky creek.

"Right, left, right," Gumbo said in his rural Florida drawl. "Easy to get to if you got the guts to do it."

Ty looked at Thane with concern. Thane winked at him and grinned before he whispered, "It's just part of the act."

Gradually, the saw grass turned to brush and then into a full-grown mangrove swamp. The creek narrowed and twisted, and the mangrove trees soon made a canopy above them that reduced the sun to a twinkling. Ty looked up at a branch of one tree and saw movement that made him blink. It was as if the bark were alive. He squinted and peered harder.

That's when Gumbo reached up and shook a branch, spilling dozens of creepy crawlers into the bottom of the boat. Ty jumped up and back from the scuttling creatures, black as coal and coming his way. The boat lurched sideways and Ty fell.

CHAPTER FORTY-SEVEN

THANE GRABBED TY BY the collar and kept him from falling overboard. The creatures scurried up over the edges of the boat and into the water.

Gumbo howled with laughter. "They's just spider crabs. Won't hurt nothin' a-tall."

Ty flicked one of the crabs off his pants leg. "Are they spiders? Or crabs?"

"Crabs that look kinda like spiders, don't ya think?" said Gumbo. "Didn't mean for you to almost go over. Sorry 'bout that."

"It's okay." Ty wanted to be polite.

Tate snatched up a spider crab and studied it before tossing it overboard and looking around at the branches above. "Wow, look at these little buggers. There's millions of them."

Ty wanted to push Gumbo out over the back, but Gumbo's face suddenly somehow got even paler. His eyes went wide and he reversed the motor with a frantic whine.

"What?" Thane asked, grabbing the edge of the boat to steady himself.

Gumbo pointed at the branches in front of them. "Now *that's* something to be scared of. Talk about maneaters. They ought to change their sign from gators to them critters."

Ty followed the direction of Gumbo's finger and blinked twice at what he saw now. Moving across the bridge of branches from one side of the creek to another was a snake as fat as a telephone pole. Juices of fear rushed up from Ty's stomach.

"What is it?" Tate asked.

"Burmese python." Gumbo spoke as if talking to himself. "They get up to a hundred and fifty pounds."

"Is it *real*?" Tate asked.

Gumbo nodded. "They's hundreds of thousands of 'em in the 'Glades nowadays. Eat everything. Got a little two-year-old girl last year. Giving the gators a run for their money."

Ty shivered as the enormous beast slithered away into the trees and wished he'd never seen the poster board in the lobby. Tate seemed fascinated, and even when they continued on into the grove, she craned her neck to follow the slithering shadow.

Finally, they came to an open pool of water. On the far side was another creek, and that seemed to lead to a high spot of ground with real trees. Ty saw the distant glint of metal, a tin roof.

"What's that over there?" Ty asked.

Gumbo glanced and shrugged. "Old Seminole fish camp. It's haunted."

"Haunted by what?" Tate's voice was full of doubt.

Gumbo shrugged again, unwavering in his story. "Pirates, bushwhackers, bootleggers. Every kind of bad man you can think of. It ain't just gators and snakes out here in the 'Glades. That's the history of it. Criminals robbin' banks and cuttin' folks' throats, then takin' to the swamp for cover. That's Florida, and these . . . are your man-eaters."

Gumbo waved an arm toward the sunny side of the open water.

At first, Ty thought they were fallen logs, but he watched close and saw the little evil eyes of the big gators. "This place is crazy."

Tate nodded at him, but clapped her hands like they were watching a good scary movie.

Gumbo reached into a bag he kept under the backseat and fished out a raw and slimy chicken wing, which he held dangling for them to see. "And now, ladies and gentlemen. The man-eaters . . ."

Gumbo tossed the chicken wing into the air in a great, curving arc. Twenty feet from the boat, before the meat hit the water, the surface exploded with spray, gnashing teeth, and the thrashing snouts of not one but three massive alligators. When one snatched the chicken from the air, the excitement didn't end. The two others attacked the first, and their tails sprayed water into the air like a rain shower until they finally disappeared into the murk.

"Awesome!" Tate said. "Can you do it again?"

Ty's fingers clenched the seat beneath him.

"Don't you want him to do it again?" Tate asked him, her face alight with the thrill of it all.

"Yeah," Ty said in a croak.

All Thane said was "Wow."

A dozen chicken wings went into the water, and the show never let up. Tate hooted with laughter and excitement while Ty's stomach did cartwheels. Finally, the bag was empty and Gumbo reached down to yank on the pull rope to start the motor. Now the gators, floating like submerged logs, completely surrounded the boat. Only the caps of their scaly gray heads and the yellow marbles of their eyes poked above the water's surface.

Blue smoke filled the air, and the motor coughed.

"Uh-oh," Gumbo said.

Ty's eyes widened at the thought of being stranded in the midst of such a horror show. "Uh-oh? Uh-oh, what?"

CHAPTER FORTY-EIGHT

"SHE'S A LITTLE FUSSY is all." Gumbo looked embarrassed. "I'd appreciate the heck out of it if y'all didn't mention this back at the hotel. They're kinda finicky about things like this. Last time I got fired, my uncle had to threaten to shut down their seafood delivery. My uncle's with the Teamsters. He knows lots of people."

"Last time you got fired?" Ty waved the blue smoke away from his face as the air cleared.

Gumbo just stood staring at the motor. "It's not that it *won't* start. She's just gotta settle down a bit. I flooded her a little."

As if on cue, thunder rumbled. Ty looked up, and sure enough, without his even noticing it, a towering wall of thunderclouds had crept into the empty sky from the south.

"How long does she have to settle?" Thane still looked relaxed about the whole thing.

"Umm, five, ten, no more than twenty."

"Minutes?" Ty asked, knowing the answer, but unable to hold his tongue.

"That'd be right," Gumbo said, still staring forlornly.

Thunder rumbled again, and the approaching clouds seemed to turn grayer by the second.

Tate looked around sadly at the gators' unblinking eyes. "Wish we had some more chicken wings."

Thane sat in the bow of the boat, lounging out with his face tilted toward the sunshine. A wind suddenly whipped through the mangroves, hissing like the collective soul of a hundred thousand Burmese pythons. Ty watched as, one by one, the gators' eyes disappeared beneath the water's rippled surface. Leaves torn from the mangroves' branches swirled around them, clicking off the boat's metal skin. Gumbo checked his watch.

Only when the sun disappeared behind the tower of thunderclouds did Thane sit up straight and look around. Fat droplets of rain began to burst all about them at random moments.

"What do you think, Gumbo?" Thane asked.

Gumbo looked at his watch. "If I do it too soon, we'll have to wait again."

Lightning flashed like a blinding white vein. Thunder cracked the sky.

"Can we get into that fish camp?" Thane nodded

toward the spot where Ty had seen the glint of a tin roof.

Gumbo's eyes went wide. He shook his head.

"Well, we gotta do something." Thane looked up at the rolling clouds.

Gumbo bent over his motor, glanced back at Thane one more time, then pulled the cord.

The motor coughed and sputtered.

As it did the first time, blue smoke filled the air.

Lightning hit so close, even Tate jumped.

The motor went quiet.

Ty closed his eyes, crossed his fingers, and said a prayer.

CHAPTER FORTY-NINE

ANOTHER PULL, AND THE motor let out a single cough, no bigger than the sound of a small child clearing his throat.

Gumbo brightened. He bent over and gave the cord still another tug.

The engine sputtered, coughed, and kept coughing. Gumbo fanned the smoke from his face and fiddled with a knob on the engine. The coughing continued, growing stronger by the second. Finally, Gumbo cranked the throttle, revving it to life with a roar that rose and fell like a siren. More raindrops fell, but after a clank of gears, the boat took off, its bow rising steadily as Gumbo made for the creek.

The mangrove canopy shielded them from the big drops. They soon hit the canal, then zipped into the other creek. When they hit the main canal, the Florida Grand glowed at them through what had become a steady rain. Ty's heart soared. Even though the bolts of lightning had grown ever closer, he knew they would outrun the most dangerous part of the storm.

Gumbo guided the boat into its slip with expert skill, reversing at just the right moment so that the boat touched the dock with a gentle kiss. They hopped out of the boat, and Tate giggled. Ty felt giddy too, now safe from the storm. Thunder crackled. Thane stuffed some money into Gumbo's hand and then led Ty and Tate across the empty pool area toward the big hotel lobby. When they arrived, they threw themselves down onto a big leather couch, soaking wet and laughing together like fools. Thunder grumbled outside, no longer a danger to them. Thane saw someone he knew from the NFL and excused himself before disappearing into another area of the huge lobby.

"Wow!" Tate said, watching Thane hobble away. "Was *that* fun!"

"I don't know how fun it was, but we got you back by dinner." Ty pointed at a clock on the lobby wall.

"Yeah, well, I'm here as Troy and his mom's guest, so you know . . ."

"Sure," Ty said, then paused. "I don't think Troy likes me too much."

Tate waved her hand in the air. "Troy's great. He likes you. He's just been through a lot lately."

"You mean the contract with the Jets?"

"And all the TV and the crazy excitement, yes, but more than that."

"That thing about him imagining he saw his dad?" Ty asked.

Tate looked around and leaned closer to Ty, lowering her voice. "Troy never knew his dad until a couple of months ago. He showed up and all of a sudden became Troy's, like, agent or something. *He* did the deal with the Jets."

"Well, that's good, right?" Ty said.

Tate shook her head. "But the dad was mixed up with some really bad people. He stole a lot of money and the FBI was after him and he just disappeared. It was brutal. Troy was crushed. Then he thought he saw him in the crowd after we won the state championship game, and since then he's thought the same thing a couple of other times. His mom is worried about him. When I asked her if it might be true—that his dad really was showing up—she said it's in Troy's mind. She says he wouldn't dare show his face because he'd be arrested."

"Would *she* have him arrested?" Ty asked.

"She's pretty bitter, and that bothers Troy, I know. I don't think Troy cares what his dad did. He misses him, and I think he'd do anything to be able to see him."

"Even imagining him?" Ty asked, but not in a mean way.

"Either way, I feel so bad for Troy. He's really sweet."

Ty didn't like to hear her talk that way about Troy, but he sure wasn't going to say so.

"Look, here they come." Tate pointed toward the lobby entrance.

Striding through the great double doors came the entire Falcons football team, returning from practice. Outside, Ty saw the last of the players streaming from two buses parked beneath the covered entryway. Beyond them, the rain hissed and lightning flashed. Ty had been around NFL players plenty with his brother, including in the locker room and on the sideline during games. Still, he never ceased to be amazed at the size of them—legs like tree trunks, heads like overturned buckets, and arms as big as holiday hams.

Tate began waving her hand frantically. In the middle of the enormous players, Troy waved back and grinned, until he saw Ty, and his expression changed to embarrassment.

"Hey," Troy said, walking up to them without sitting down, "what's going on?"

Tate recounted their adventure with the man-eaters, Gumbo's boat, and the thunderstorm.

"Great," Troy said, but Ty could tell by his tone that Troy wasn't happy about Tate spending time with him and his brother. "Well, I gotta get changed. You too, Tate. We've got dinner with the team and then the sponsor party if this rain quits. Good luck tomorrow, Ty."

With a wave, they both were gone.

Ty watched them move through the crowded lobby toward the elevators, disappointed to see Tate go and wondering if Troy had forgotten about his mom inviting Thane and him to the sponsor party, too. He watched to see if Tate would give him another wave, waiting until the elevator doors closed, but she never looked back. Ty sighed and sat staring until the doors of the elevator right next to Tate's parted, allowing a lone man to step out into the lobby.

Ty jumped to his feet.

The man was quickly swallowed up by the crowded lobby. Ty moved behind one of the massive marble columns and scanned the entire area, seeing no sign of the man. His breathing finally slowed until he felt the sudden grip of a hand on his shoulder.

CHAPTER FIFTY

"WHAT ARE YOU DOING?"

Ty caught his breath. "Thane, I think I saw him."

"Who?"

"Him. Bennie the Blade. The Blade. The killer who works for Big Al."

Thane's face fell. "Come on. Stop goofing with me."

"I'm *not* goofing." Ty looked around nervously. "I saw him. He looks like a science teacher who needs some sleep. I could never forget that face and that orange hair."

"Did he see you?" Thane looked around now, too.

"I don't think so," Ty said.

"I mean, maybe you saw him, buddy." Thane looked directly at Ty. "But maybe you didn't. This place is a zoo."

"What if that was him, following you on the beach?" Ty said, his mind spinning.

"Naw," Thane said, waving his hand in the air. "Why follow me on the beach? It doesn't make sense. I mean, there's no reason he'd be here for anything that has to do with me or you. We don't have anything to do with the teams playing Sunday, or anything that's going on besides a Seven-on-Seven tournament and some NFL parties. So . . ."

Ty almost pointed out that maybe people were gambling on his 7-on-7 tournament, but the idea was so foolish that he hung his head. "I'm just a stupid chicken, I swear."

"Hey, you're not a chicken." Thane put a hand on his shoulder. "You're my man. You're a heck of a football player. You're . . . I don't know, sensitive. And you've been through a lot."

"Scared of shadows in the dark." Ty wanted to vomit. "Scared of man-eaters, lightning bolts, snakes . . . heck, I might as well be scared of my own shadow."

"Ty, what happened with Lucy and Al D'Amico would give grown-ups nightmares." Thane tightened his grip. "You know what Mrs. Brennan said."

Mrs. Brennan was the school psychologist Ty had seen ever since arriving at Halpern Middle. Originally, Ty saw her because of the trauma of losing both his parents in a car accident. Later, she tried to help him with everything that happened with the mob and the FBI. Ty liked Mrs. Brennan, but he was embarrassed to talk about her, even with Thane, so he just shook his head.

"And that snake? It freaked me out, too," Thane said. "Who wouldn't have been scared of that big hog?"

"Tate."

"She's a pistol, I'll admit. But you've been through a lot. I'll keep my eyes open. Just stick with me. You know I've got your back."

"And I've got yours." Ty bore his eyes into Thane's.

Thane grinned at him. "Saved me from Lucy, didn't you? You were like my bodyguard, pushing him down that escalator. Okay, listen, this is what else I can do. Agent Sutherland is coming down for the big game, right? I can give him a call and have him check around. If the FBI is on these guys like he said they were, then my bet is that they'll know if the Blade is down here in Miami. Come on, let's go get out of these swamp clothes."

When they got to the room, Thane took out his cell phone and dialed up Agent Sutherland. Thane's eyes brightened and he looked at Ty as he spoke. "Agent Sutherland? Yeah, it's me, Tiger. Yeah, you can do something for me. I'm here with Ty and he thinks he might have seen one of those D'Amico guys. Bennie the Blade, the redhead who looks like a science teacher."

Thane paused to listen before he said, "Ty's worried they're after him."

Ty scowled at his older brother for his lighthearted tone with the FBI agent.

"Yes, I know," Thane said, winking at Ty. "I will tell him that. Thanks, Agent Sutherland. . . . You too. Good-bye."

"Is he down here?" Ty asked.

"*If* he's down here, and it's a big if, then it's got nothing to do with you and me," Thane said. "Sutherland was sure of that. He said the only thing is that this game being the biggest gambling event in the world, it naturally attracts all the big gamblers. That's the mob guys."

"How is he so sure?" Ty asked, still scowling.

"Ty, I don't know. You think he's hiding the truth? Come on."

Ty couldn't think of anything more to say, but he still didn't feel great.

"You want to get something to eat before you have your team meeting?" Thane asked.

Ty realized he hadn't eaten much of anything all day, so after they'd changed, they went to the hotel restaurant and had chilled stone crab claws with mustard sauce. Ty was about to head to Salon G for his team meeting when Thane told him he was going to attend a Players Association party at a hotel in Miami Beach and that he'd meet Ty later in the room.

"What about the Falcons sponsor party?" Ty asked. "With Tate and Troy's mom and meeting Seth Halloway?"

Thane seemed to have forgotten. "Well, let's see what time we're both done."

"But you told them we'd go."

"Ty, people say they'll stop by or go to things like that all the time. They won't miss us. It's going to be a huge thing. Don't worry—when I get back, if you're done and it's still happening, we'll go down for a few minutes."

"Can't you just stay here and wait?" Ty knew by his brother's tone that the sponsor party wasn't looking good for them, and he wanted another chance to see Tate. "The Players Association? You don't have to do that, do you?"

"Are you worried about that Blade guy you thought you saw?" Thane asked. "I should be back before you're out of film. I bet that goes late. If I'm wrong, you can just go from your meeting back to the room and wait for me. I won't be late. Relax. It's only a party. There'll be more."

The coaches were already in Salon G, running film of their next opponents back and forth, a team from Tulsa. The coaches talked about what plays they thought would work and debated the strengths and weaknesses of individual players based on what they saw. Ty watched and listened and turned his mind to football to forget about the party and the girl.

When all the players had arrived, Coach Bavaro put on the lights and stood in front of them with a big white greaseboard. Using a black marker, he drew up the Raptors offense with Os, then the Tulsa players with Xs.

"If we line up in trips," Coach Bavaro said, pointing to the three wide receivers loaded up on the right side of the ball, "then they'll lock this backside guy up, man to man. Then, if we shift over before the snap and leave the single receiver to the right . . ."

Coach Bavaro wiped two of the Os off the board before adding them to the other side and using arrows to show how the Xs would follow.

"The locked-on man coverage will be here, to the right, and it'll be with their worst cornerback, number twenty-six."

The coach turned and looked at Ty. "Ty, you'll be the Z on this. Twenty-six will have man coverage on you."

Coach Bavaro turned back to the board. He put the point of the marker down in the middle of Ty's O, then drew a line straight up the board, capping it with an arrow.

"Touchdown." The coach grinned. "No way can this kid cover you."

Coach Bavaro used a towel to wipe the board clean, talking as he worked. "Now, we've got other things we'll do, but shifting into a trips formation and having Ty run a go route against twenty-six? That's going to be our bread and butter. We'll win or lose tomorrow based on that play."

The coach turned back to face the team. "So, Ty, you ready?"

CHAPTER FIFTY-ONE

ALL WEEK, TY WAS ready. He didn't mind missing the Falcons sponsor party because the extra film work paid off. He caught eighteen touchdowns in five games. The team spent most of its free time not at the pool or taking trips to the beach, but holed up in Salon G, watching film and going over plays on the greaseboard. Coach Bavaro was maniacal with his preparation, but the players couldn't complain because it was all working. Ty didn't complain because it kept his mind off of the Blade, the D'Amico family, and the FBI.

The one distraction their hard work didn't eliminate was Tate. Two times during the week when the team was given an hour to relax after lunch, Ty had seen Tate by the pool. Even though Troy White and his mom had Tate sandwiched between them, Ty approached her, stammering and mumbling in an effort to spark a conversation. Both times, Troy wore a blank stare and, although he said hello, he seemed to be in another world, and one where Ty wasn't welcome. Tate's obvious discomfort finally won out, and Ty wandered away to swim with his teammates and steal glances at Tate and her friends.

It wasn't that Ty's entire week was ruined, though. He knew that if the team's hard work paid off, they'd be playing on Super Bowl Sunday, right in the Dolphins' stadium the morning of the Super Bowl itself. Before the Falcons and Patriots even got to see the field that day, Ty and the Raptors would have played for a title of their own.

Going into Friday's semifinal game against the Northern California Knights, Ty felt confident. With the same thorough film study and strategy sessions that Coach Bavaro said NFL teams used, Ty and the Raptors seemed to be one step ahead of their competition. Ty had to wonder, however, if their coach had even considered what would happen if they made it to the finals.

Troy White's Georgia team kept winning, too, and they also seemed destined for the finals. Ty wondered how even the Raptors' NFL-style preparation could be a match against a kid like Troy White, who would supposedly know the plays they'd run before the ball was even snapped. Ty worried that nothing could defeat that.

Friday morning arrived with a windy, overcast sky spitting droplets of rain like watermelon seeds. Ty warmed up with his team and didn't notice Tate in the stands until the captains went out for the coin toss. Ty began to wave but hesitated when he saw Troy's game face directed right at him. Ty dropped his hand to his side and focused on the field, knowing that Troy wasn't there to cheer him on. He was there to scout both teams, knowing that whoever won would play the Georgia team on Super Bowl Sunday if Georgia won later in the day.

The Raptors won the toss, and Ty took the field with his offense. As expected, Northern California's fastest cornerback, a kid named Morris Lasheen, number twenty, lined up across from Ty. What Ty didn't expect as he ran his first route, a deep post pattern, was for the safety to drop immediately into the deep zone. They were double-covering him. Ty ran his route, but as fast as he was, with the double coverage there was no way to get open. The Raptors completed a seven-yard swing pass to the running back, and Ty jogged back to the huddle.

"They doubled me." Ty looked at David Bavaro as he stepped into the huddle.

"I know," the quarterback said. "Let's see what they do this time; we'll go trips away from you."

Ty knew that if they were to double-team him with the three other wide receivers on the other side of the field, it would make it very hard to cover all three as well as the running back. The Raptors broke the huddle, and he ran up to the line, ready to run a go route, straight up the field for the end zone. Lasheen lined up across from him, and the safety began to rotate his way, setting up a deep zone. Ty thought that maybe the safety would roll back the other way once the ball was snapped, but that wasn't what happened.

Ty took off, and the safety stayed over the top of him, making it impossible for him to use his speed to get deep, and letting Lasheen, the speedy cornerback, play any break Ty might make underneath without having to worry about the deep ball. Ty gritted his teeth, even as he ran.

Northern California kept it up, doubling him the entire game. Even when the Raptors took the lead, they didn't relent in their commitment to stopping Ty. Late in the game, Coach Bavaro put an arm around Ty's shoulders on the sideline.

"Great job out there," he said.

"I don't have a catch," Ty said.

"But we're winning because they're worried about getting beat deep by you. It's not a bad strategy, shutting you down with that deep zone."

"It's a terrible strategy." Ty stole a glance into the stands, first at his brother, then briefly at Tate. "I look like I'm useless."

"Not to anyone who knows the game. We're going to

get into the championship. That's what we came here for. You're helping to make it happen, Ty, just by being out there."

"This sure doesn't feel like football to me."

"Hang in there, buddy. You'll get your chances. It's not always balloons and candy bars."

"You don't think Georgia will do the same thing to me?" Ty asked.

"I doubt it," Coach Bavaro said.

"Why?"

Coach Bavaro looked up into the stands himself, and Ty knew that he was looking at Troy White. "Thing is, I don't know if they're going to think they have to double-cover you or anybody. Not with that kid up there."

"Troy White?"

Bavaro nodded.

"You think he's for real?" Ty asked.

"I know he is."

CHAPTER FIFTY-TWO

AFTER THE RAPTORS' VICTORY, Coach Bavaro insisted the entire team stay and watch the other semifinal game.

"We'll dig into the film tonight," Bavaro said, "but I want you guys to see them in real time. Watch the guys who you're going to have to cover, or the guys who'll be covering you. It's great that we're playing on Super Bowl Sunday, but boys, there's only one team in the whole country that gets to go home a winner, and that's gonna be us."

There was time before the next game, and one of the coaches showed up with several boxes of pizza and a couple of cases of soda. The team members and their families found a spot on one of the practice fields, where they ate their lunch and reveled in their victory.

"You know we're going to be on ESPN Two?" David

Bavaro asked several of the players.

Ty felt the thrill of being on TV, then remembered there really wasn't anyone who would watch for him. He had a fleeting notion of trying to get word to Charlotte. She'd watch, but Charlotte was living another life in another city, someplace Ty would never see. He looked over at his brother, who was swapping football stories with Coach Bavaro and Michael Strahan, and his heart ached. It was just the two of them. That was all it would ever be, and although Ty was eternally grateful to have his brother, Thane, it somehow seemed unsafe to have an entire family made up of only two people. It seemed like a lot of pressure, maybe too much to be healthy.

Ty sighed and got to his feet, wandering over toward the fence, from which he could see the Georgia team already warming up against their opponents from Dallas. Receivers ran deep passing routes while Troy dropped perfect bombs into their hands.

David Bavaro joined him at the fence. "You think Dallas can beat them?"

Ty shrugged. "Anybody can beat anybody, right? That's why you play the game."

"True," Bavaro said.

Soon the others were ready, and the team moved back into the stands to watch. The stands filled steadily until not a seat remained and the crowd spilled around the edges of the field outside the fence. The wind picked up as the Georgia offense took the field. Dallas was bigger and faster, and they hung on all the way until the end, when Troy ripped off three unanswered touchdown passes in a row.

After the final whistle, the Georgia team raised Troy up on their shoulders and marched around the field chanting, "Super Sunday, Super Sunday, Super Sunday." Ty looked at Coach Bavaro's face, unmoving as a statue's until he blinked and got up out of his seat, turning to the team. "Guys, you take the rest of the day off, and let us get this film broken down. We've got all day tomorrow to get ready for Sunday. We'll start early with film at eight and then practice after lunch. Make sure you get yourselves to bed tonight at a decent hour. Okay, see you tomorrow morning at eight. Congratulations."

Ty and Thane returned to the hotel and changed into their bathing suits.

"Should I bring a ball?" Thane asked.

"Nah," Ty said, showing him a book. "Let's just sit by the pool."

"Okay. You deserve a rest." Thane swapped his football for a book on the bedside table.

They rode down in the elevator with a couple of teammates and their parents, and everyone still chattered excitedly about the next day and playing on TV. The pool area was crowded and noisy, but Thane spotted a couple of chairs over by the beach. As they spread some towels on the chairs, Ty saw Tate by the pool. There was a chair next to her with a towel on it, but Tate was alone. Finally.

Ty lost his breath, but he bit into his lower lip and told Thane he'd be back in a few minutes.

Thane looked in the direction Ty was staring and said, "Oh, I get it. Good. Go for it, buddy."

Ty wanted to ask her if she'd friend him on Facebook. There was something about her that made Ty determined to override his fear of her saying no.

He circled the pool without her seeing him. She lay much as she had four days ago, with sunglasses on, listening to an iPod.

Ty walked right up to her.

He stood at the bottom of her chair. His shadow darkened her face. Tate removed her sunglasses and sat up.

CHAPTER FIFTY-THREE

"Good." Ty's tongue tangled and nothing more came out. Everything he thought of saying, everything he wanted to ask her, now seemed foolish and lame.

"So, what are you doing?" Tate shielded her eyes from the sun with one hand.

Ty shrugged. He stuffed his hands into the pockets of his bathing suit and looked down at his feet. Tate laughed softly, and he looked up at her.

"You're just standing there," she said.

Ty swallowed and cleared his throat, summoning up all his courage, knowing that this might be his last chance. Tomorrow he would be practicing all day and then Sunday morning was the 7-on-7 championship. After that, the Super Bowl itself. Things would be crazy and people would be everywhere. Tate might be traveling with the team, for all Ty knew, and she might be headed home on a charter flight right after the big game. If he didn't say something now, he might never see her again for the rest of his life and he was sure he'd always regret that, no matter what happened.

"I . . ." Ty began to speak, but stopped when he realized someone now stood beside him.

"Hey," Troy said, and not in a friendly way. "What's up?"

"We were just talking," Tate said.

Ty looked from Troy to Tate and back again.

"Look what I got, Tate," Troy said, holding up two big tickets. "Platinum tickets for the Falcons VIP party tonight. Toby Keith and Beyoncé are going to be there. How good is that?"

"Wow." Tate swung her legs off the chair and stood up to take one of the tickets. "This is so cool."

"I know, and Beyoncé is going to do a sound check in about ten minutes. If we show them these tickets, we can watch. You want to?"

"Awesome," Tate said, then she looked at Ty and smiled. "If I don't see you, I hope you do good Sunday, Ty. Even though you know how I think it'll turn out. It was nice meeting you."

"Yeah." Troy acted like a puppet with someone else pulling the strings when he extended his hand to shake Ty's. "Good luck, Ty. Nice meeting you. Maybe I'll see you up in New York."

Ty said nothing as he watched them gather up their

things. Tate waved again and said good-bye before heading for the hotel, and still, all Ty could do was silently return the wave. When they disappeared from sight, Ty shuffled back to where Thane sat.

"How'd it go?" Thane lay back in his chair, facing the sun. Only his lips moved, and it sounded like he might have dozed off.

Ty sat down in the chair next to his brother and put his face into his hands.

"What's wrong?" Thane asked. "Everything okay?"

"Thane, do you think there's any way you could get tickets for the Falcons VIP party tonight?"

"That platinum ticket thing?" Thane asked.

"I guess."

"Man, Ty," Thane said, scratching his ear, "that's just for the Falcons and a couple of real big shots. I heard Beyoncé is going to be there."

"I know. Can you?"

"I doubt it."

Ty bit into his lower lip.

"But, for you? I'll sure try."

CHAPTER FIFTY-FOUR

THANE STARTED DIALING UP friends and acquaintances. He called his agent. He called teammates. He called players he knew from college all-star teams, and even a couple of people in the media. No one had platinum tickets. Finally, Thane snapped his phone shut and shrugged.

"I don't know, buddy. Sorry."

Ty tried not to let his disappointment show. He tried to cling to the hope that he'd somehow see Tate during the day tomorrow, or after the championship game, even though he knew it was highly unlikely. Even if he did, chances were they wouldn't be able to talk.

"Maybe I'll just hang out in the lobby and see if I see anyone there," Thane said.

"Want me to come?" Ty asked.

"No, I'm better alone. You just sit."

Thane left Ty alone with his book, but Ty couldn't concentrate. He kept looking at his watch and wondering what Thane was doing. He looked around the pool himself, desperate for a face he might know who could possibly have extra tickets. The more time went by, the more desperate Ty began to feel. Finally, he took out his phone, looked in his contacts for Agent Sutherland, and dialed his cell phone.

"Ty Lewis?" Agent Sutherland said.

"Hi, Agent Sutherland. Yes, it's me. I'm sorry to call you."

"Ty, I told your brother: I have no idea if the Blade is in Miami. You didn't think you saw him again, did you?"

"No, I'm not calling about that."

"No? Oh. What's up?"

"Well, you're down here in Miami for the game, right?"

"Yes."

"You aren't by chance going to that platinum party with Beyoncé, are you?"

Sutherland snorted and laughed. "Are you kidding? How would I be going to that?"

"I thought the FBI might be doing, like, security or something."

"It's Beyoncé, not the president."

Ty felt silly. "Oh."

Sutherland laughed again. "Tell your brother again how much I appreciate the tickets, will you? Sorry I couldn't help, Ty."

"I'll tell him, but, uh, Agent Sutherland? Do you think we could keep this conversation between you and me? I feel kind of stupid."

"You got it," Sutherland said, "and the only stupid question is the one you don't ask. That's what I always say. You keep your eyes open, Ty."

"What do you mean? Why?"

"I don't mean anything. Just an expression."

Ty thanked him and hung up, just as Thane appeared, circling the pool and heading his way. Thane flopped down in his chair and folded his arms across his chest. He wore an expression Ty just couldn't read.

Ty asked, "Well?"

CHAPTER FIFTY-FIVE

THANE REACHED INTO THE deep side pocket of his bathing suit and flipped two glimmering tickets into view.

"You got them!" Ty jumped right up out of his seat. He high-fived Thane over and over, alternating one hand and the other.

"Easy, easy." Thane laughed.

Ty stopped and took the tickets and examined them. "How?"

"I wasn't kidding when I told you there was no way I could get them, but who did I see in the lobby? Mr. Cole."

"The owner?"

Thane nodded. "He pulled them out of his coat pocket like they were two sticks of chewing gum and gave them to me like nothing."

"You're kidding!"

"Yeah, I guess his wife—you know his wife's the big singer, Helena, right?"

"Yeah."

"Yeah, well, I guess her plane got stuck in Europe somewhere and she can't make it back for the party. He told me he just got off the phone with her and he didn't want to go alone. How about that for luck?"

"It's great." Ty couldn't keep from beaming.

"We'll have to get you something fancy to wear."

Ty looked down at his faded bathing suit. "I thought we didn't care what we looked like."

"Not usually," Thane said. "But this is really big."

"Brett Favre was really big."

"Not like Beyoncé, though."

"He is to me."

"Well, I'll tell Favre when I see him, or you can. Anyway, let's go get something so we look the part. I don't want us using the owner's tickets and showing up looking like Uncle Gus."

"We never look like him."

"But you know what I'm getting at. Look, see?" Thane pointed to the ticket. "It says 'formal attire'— that's a suit and tie. Come on, we'll go to that Weston Town Center. They'll have something there, I think. We'll arrive in style."

They changed out of their bathing suits and went to the Weston Town Center, where they bought clothes

Ty normally thought of as stiff and uncomfortable, but weren't.

"I can't believe how this feels," Ty said that evening as they got ready for the party. He smoothed the leg of his pants and tugged on a jacket sleeve. "I always thought a suit and tie was like getting wrapped up in sandpaper and duct tape."

Thane laughed and fidgeted with his tie in the mirror. "When you get the right stuff, it's supposed to be comfortable. Mom just bought whatever was on sale at Marshalls and stuck us in it. Didn't hurt us any, though, did it?"

Ty's throat tightened at the mention of their mom. He could almost smell the strawberry shampoo she always used and feel her long, cool fingers against his cheek. The room was silent for a minute before Thane said, "Sorry. I know you miss them."

"Don't you?"

Thane crossed the room and hugged Ty to him, resting his chin on Ty's head. "Sometimes I forget they're gone. Sometimes I think that's a good thing, just pretending that it never happened."

"I wish it didn't." Ty felt the tears welling up in his eyes.

Thane squeezed him even tighter. "I know, buddy. I know."

Thane separated from Ty and put his hands on Ty's shoulders. "She'd be proud of us now, though, right? You and me decked out like a couple of GQ models?"

Ty had to laugh. Any time they'd complained about the clothes they were given growing up, their mom had always responded by saying, "What do you think you are, a GQ model or something? Just wear it."

Thane turned Ty around so that they both faced the mirror in their dressy clothes.

"We look good," Ty said.

"So, let's go." Thane clapped his hands.

CHAPTER FIFTY-SIX

THE ELEVATOR WAS FILLED with people dressed for the party as well, women in glittering gowns and men in tuxedos. Ty looked at his own yellow necktie and straightened it a bit. Thane winked at him and grinned. They moved with the fancy crowd through the hotel lobby and toward the entrance to the gardens. Ty hadn't seen them before, but he was impressed when they walked outside and down a red carpet. A fat yellow moon looked down from above. Only a tatter of ghostly clouds blotted the stars. Towering on either side of the garden entrance were spiral bushes reaching for the night sky. The rest of the hedges had been cut so tightly that it was hard to imagine they were real. Flowers along the path exploded with color.

Thane presented their tickets and in they went,

through an archway woven with yellow roses perfuming the warm, gentle breeze. At the center of everything was a long and narrow reflecting pool. Beyond it, maybe twenty tables with chairs draped in white fabric. Beyond that was a stage whose backdrop looked like an enormous seashell. Different-colored lights shone on the spot where Ty presumed Beyoncé and Toby Keith would play. Off to one side, a woman sat strumming a harp. The peaceful notes seemed to float on the breeze. Grass as smooth and thick as carpet bordered the reflecting pool. A bar for drinks flanked either side, backed up by more hedges and trees beyond that.

"Let's look around," Thane said, and Ty followed.

Pathways of small white stones ran throughout the garden, where statues and gurgling fountains stood among jungle trees, rainforest flowers, and twisty shrubs. The sights and smells and sounds made Ty pinch himself. They wandered through the gardens, running into random pairs of people. Some were obviously Falcons players. Jon Abraham appeared and recognized Thane, calling him Tiger as most people did. Thane introduced Ty, and his hand disappeared inside the defensive end's grip. They kept going but saw no sign of Tate.

Finally, they emerged through an opening in the hedge along the reflecting pool just beside one of the bars.

"You want a soda or something?" Thane asked.

"I guess," Ty said.

"Okay, I'll be back." Thane disappeared into the little crowd of people at the bar.

Ty turned away and looked at the people along his side of the pool, and that was when he saw Tate.

She looked very pretty with her hair piled up atop her head and woven with small white flowers. On either side of her stood Troy and Troy's mom. Ty felt a different kind of lump in his throat from the one he'd had over his mother. Ty waited and watched through the crowd. When Troy's mom and Tate began talking to what looked like a Falcons player and Troy began talking to a man who looked like a coach, Ty made his move.

He left his spot and walked right up to Tate and tapped her shoulder. "Hi. Hey, in case I don't see you, I wanted to ask if I could friend you on Facebook. Maybe I could even get your cell phone number."

Tate turned her head. Her mouth fell open like she didn't know what to say.

"Can I have your number?" Ty persisted.

Tate told him her number, speaking over her shoulder, and Ty punched it into his phone with great satisfaction even though Tate had already turned her attention back to the player.

Troy turned away from the coach he'd been talking to and stared at Ty in disbelief for a moment before he asked, "What did you just say to her?"

CHAPTER FIFTY-SEVEN

TY DIDN'T GET A chance to answer.

Before he could squeeze a single word from his mouth, Troy's eyes slipped past Ty and his face lost all expression. Ty recalled the look Troy had worn in the restaurant on Lincoln Road. Troy sprang forward so quickly that Ty winced.

But Troy never touched Ty. He simply skirted past and kept going without a word. Ty turned and followed Troy with his eyes as he darted through the crowd.

Troy stopped at the corner of the tall hedge beyond the reflecting pool. A tall, handsome man wearing a tuxedo put a hand on Troy's shoulder, grinning widely. When the two of them disappeared around the corner of the hedge, Ty turned to see that both Tate and Troy's mom had their backs to him, still in deep conversation with the Falcons player.

Curiosity overwhelmed Ty, and without thinking he took off after Troy. He rounded the corner of the hedge and saw the last glimpse of Troy as he and the tall man stepped into the opening of another hedge at the far side of a wide flower garden. Under the heavy moon, the dark shapes of two more grown-ups followed close behind. Ty had no idea who they were or where they'd come from but could only think of a nature show he'd seen where two snakes followed a mouse back into its hole.

Ty looked back and saw no sign of Thane in the crowd. Tate and Troy's mom still didn't seem to know he or Troy had gone. Ty set aside caution and kept going. He wasn't going to make a fool out of himself by running back to his big brother, scared of every little shadow. He could only presume the man Troy was with was his father, and even though he was a wanted man, he didn't sound so bad. Ty would scope things out before he alerted anyone else. If Troy was with his father and Ty ruined it, Tate was as likely to despise Ty as Troy was.

When Ty reached the far side of the garden, he saw that the hedges had been cut into a maze that looked like it went on quite some way. Ty took a breath and stepped inside with only the moon to light his path. He turned and twisted and tried to keep moving in the direction of the moon. Each shadow startled him. He heard a noise, froze, and changed his mind, confused at how he'd ever let his feet carry him this far. He was lost.

Ty whispered aloud to himself. "What am I doing?"

The man Troy was with might be his father, but if that was true, that same man was wanted by the FBI. He was a fugitive. The two men following them could be anybody. Whether Troy and Tate hated him for intruding or not, the smart thing was to go back and get some help.

That's what he should have done from the beginning, but it all had happened so fast, and his mind had been spinning. Now, lost and alone, Ty headed back in the direction of the party's noise. He turned several corners and thought he had only returned to the same spot. When he heard the low voices of two men just through the hedge, he froze. The voices moved, and Ty realized they were heading his way. Just before they rounded the corner, Ty took off.

He ran with every ounce of speed he had, no longer paying attention to the moon or the sound of the party, only trying to distance himself from the men. Running full tilt, he scratched his face and arms as he cut the corners of the hedges. When he saw an opening in the maze up ahead, he took off for it and bolted free from the prison of shrubs and into an empty space, where he tripped and landed on his face in a patch of grass.

Even as he fell, he realized where he was. The

marina's hut squatted next to the boats like an ogre, and the moonlight glittered off the rippling water.

Ty scrambled to his feet the instant he went down, with the intention of running for the pool area, but he was too late. The two men sprang from the maze and pounced on him like cats. They gripped his arms, and the sight of their faces sent a shiver of fear through Ty's frame that left him limp, helpless, and silent.

Bennie the Blade wore the small smirk of a killer on his face, but that didn't scare Ty as much as the other face. White teeth glowed from the mouth of Big Al's nephew. Pete Bonito leaned close to Ty, breathing heavy and leaving the taste of sardines, alcohol, and hair gel in the air. His jet-black flattop glistened and his bug eyes bulged.

Both men were dressed for the party in tuxedos.

"Well, look what we got here." Bonito's voice was gruff, deep, and raspy. "It's that kid we wanted to talk to a couple weeks ago, ain't it, Zipper?"

They tightened their grips on Ty's arms.

Soft and sure came Bennie the Blade's voice. "Yeah, it is. It's that kid."

CHAPTER FIFTY-EIGHT

BENNIE THE BLADE TOOK out a roll of duct tape and expertly bound Ty's wrists. He then tore off a stubby rectangular piece that he plastered across Ty's mouth. Ty's eyes went wide with fear as the mobsters lifted him off his feet and carried him toward the dock. They rounded the corner of the thatch-roofed shack toward the boat slips. Ty was certain they were going to throw him in, until he saw Troy's face staring up at him from the seat in the middle of Gumbo's swamp boat.

Ty hadn't imagined he could ever feel so glad to see Troy White, but he was. Somehow, he felt like Troy's presence would keep them from tossing him into the dark water.

"What are you doing to him?" Troy obviously wasn't the least bit afraid of these men. His voice was demanding and insulted.

"Easy, kid," Bonito said. "He's just gonna take a little ride with you and your dad because this kid just can't keep his nose out of other people's business."

"Take that off his mouth," Troy said, pointing at Ty's gag. "What's wrong with you?"

Bonito put a finger to his lips. "Shhh. You don't want your dad going to jail, do you? We got to keep your buddy here quiet if you want to have a little father-and-son time together. That's what you want, don't you?"

The man standing in the back of the boat with his hand on the motor's long arm quickly turned around. He nodded at Troy, signaling for him to agree with Bonito. Ty studied the man in the boat. He was handsome, with thick eyebrows and the weatherworn face of a cowboy, a big man with long, thick limbs. He wore a tuxedo. On his wrist was a slim gold watch. There was no mistaking his relationship with Troy. He was the man the FBI was after. The man who stole a lot of money. The man who was mixed up with some really bad people.

Ty looked at Bonito and the Blade and wondered if Troy had any idea how bad.

"It's okay, Troy." Troy's dad turned to start the motor. "Your friend will be fine."

Troy looked at Ty with concern and didn't deny Ty was his friend. Ty wondered why but was thankful for it because he felt like it might keep these men from doing something bad to him.

"Drew, your kid's phone." Bonito motioned his chin toward Troy.

Drew held out his hand. "Troy, I need your cell phone."

"Why?"

"Troy, please. We don't have time for me to explain right now. I need it. It's very important."

Troy reluctantly took the cell phone from his pants pocket and handed it to his dad. His dad handed it to Bonito before returning his attention to the outboard motor and yanking its pull cord. The motor coughed blue smoke, but caught and raced with a high-pitched whine until Troy's dad backed off the gas. The mobsters took a quick look around, then hustled Ty into the boat, seating him next to Troy and shoving the boat off into the water. Ty inhaled sharply, then breathed a sigh of relief through his nose as the distance between them and the mobsters grew. The two men in tuxedos turned and crossed the grass, then disappeared, not in the direction of the party, but toward the parking lot.

"You said we could get a pizza and hang out. Why are we going into the swamp?" Troy spoke accusingly to his father.

"Sh." Drew put a finger to his lips the same way Bonito had. "I've already got the pizza. Let me get us away from here, and we'll talk. You don't want me to get caught, do you?"

They rode in silence with the moonlight guiding the way. Troy stared at his father, and his facial expressions went back and forth between admiration and anger. Ty wondered at the sight they must make, two boys in suits and ties riding through the Everglades in a swamp boat driven by an outlaw in a tuxedo.

They went right, then left, then right again, and that's when Ty began to choke with fear. He knew now why they hadn't simply tossed him into the water near the dock. People would find a dead kid floating there, but they wouldn't find him floating in a deep dark pool of man-eaters. They wouldn't find anything, not even the scraps.

As they eased through the last bit of the creek, Ty had no fear left for the spider crabs scuttling across the branches overhead and occasionally dropping into the boat. His fear was focused on the wide pool of alligators up ahead.

When they emerged from the mangroves into the black pool, Ty instinctively moved away from Troy's dad.

Troy's dad let up on the gas.

"Hey," he said, "easy, kid. You'll tip us all in. Hey, kid. Cut it out."

Troy's dad reached for Ty, but Ty escaped to the front of the boat.

"Come here, kid."

Troy's dad grabbed the edges of the boat and climbed

over the middle seat, past Troy, and headed steadily toward Ty. Ty had backed himself all the way into the bow of the boat when something thrashed in the water behind him.

Troy's father growled angrily and reached for Ty.

CHAPTER FIFTY-NINE

TROY'S DAD GRABBED THE lapels of Ty's jacket. Ty felt the empty space behind him. He twisted and lost his footing, but Troy's dad yanked him back into the boat with tremendous strength, and Ty landed on the floor of the metal boat, bottom first, with a thud.

"Be careful. Are you crazy? Stop rocking. There's gators in this water."

Ty nodded his head that he knew and groaned through the tape.

"Let me get that off you." Troy's dad slowly peeled back the tape from Ty's mouth.

"Are you throwing me in?" The words squeaked out of Ty's mouth.

Troy's dad laughed. "Why would you think that?"

Ty shrugged. "They tied me up."

"They're just nervous, and a little heavy-handed. Don't worry. I've got some sodas and pizza for you guys in the fish shack, an Xbox, too. Just sit still."

Troy's dad returned to the motor, opened the throttle, and cruised across the pool of man-eaters with the metal boat's flat bottom slapping the water's ripples. Troy looked at Ty, raised his hands up, and gave Ty an apologetic look.

At the back of the pool, a channel opened up into more mangroves, but on one side the fringe of an island soon appeared. The fish camp had been built at the very edge of the channel so that as they pulled up alongside its dock, they could see up into the second-story windows, black and empty as the sockets of a skull. The siding of the camp hadn't seen a coat of paint in twenty years, if it had seen one at all. The graying wood suffered from mold, moss, and white streaks of bird poop. The fish shack was the same Seminole fish camp Gumbo had spoken of, and Ty wondered if Troy's dad knew the history of its criminal past.

They pulled in with the nose of the boat facing the island. The dock provided access to the fish camp door and led to a dirt path that disappeared into the island's thick growth of trees.

As scary as the whole thing was, Ty looked up at the moon, thankful for its yellow glow. They got out and Ty moved cautiously along the dock, whose boards seemed soft and ready to give way any second. He was relieved to finally step across the threshold and into the camp. Troy's dad hit a switch. Somewhere from the trees Ty heard a motor fire up. He knew it was the sound of a generator when the lights flickered on.

Gray plywood floors opened up into a kitchen area and a great room separated by a long plank table. A sagging couch with fat matching chairs filled the room with the smell of mold. On the walls, gator skins hung along with stuffed fish and bird feathers of every kind. The treasure of wildlife trophies included a yellow-eyed black jaguar in one corner, flanked by a skunk, an armadillo, a turkey, and the skin of what Ty knew must have been one of the giant Burmese pythons. Even the memory of that massive snake made him shudder.

On the floor not too far from the couch sat a flat-screen TV, fresh from its box, along with an Xbox and two red controllers.

"Well?" Troy's dad said, heading for the kitchen. "It's not home, but it'll do for what we need."

"Need for what?" Troy asked his father.

Troy's father clapped his hands together and rubbed them as if he were cold. "Let me get that pizza and some drinks, and we'll get everything all straight. Don't you worry about a thing. This is gonna work out great and everyone will be happy. I promise. Go ahead, you two sit down at the table."

Ty sat.

"What about the tape on Ty's wrists?" Troy asked.

Troy's father looked up from the box of pizza he had opened. "Uh, let's just leave that for now. No offense, but I don't want my partners showing up and making a fuss. They get irritated pretty easily, and I'm not even sure how they're going to handle me taking the tape off his mouth."

Troy gave Ty another apologetic look. Troy's father plunked down paper plates loaded with cheese slices in front of them along with two cans of soda before he sat at the head of the table with a look of satisfaction. "There, that'll fill you up."

Ty felt suddenly starved. He looked at Troy before using his bound-up hands to guide a slice of pie into his mouth, chewing greedily and swallowing before using both hands to take a slug of soda that left him burping.

Troy didn't touch the food. He stared intently at his father. "I'm not hungry."

"Come on. Kids love pizza." Troy's father took a bite of his own and wiped a string of cheese from his chin. "You said you'd love to have some and hang out."

"No, Dad. There's something more. I get not letting Ty go back and tell anyone, but keeping his hands taped up? I want to know what's going on. I don't care who those guys are, you don't just kidnap my friend."

The word hung in the air. The sound of it startled Ty. It was true.

He had been kidnapped.

CHAPTER SIXTY

"NOBODY'S KIDNAPPING ANYONE," TROY'S dad said. "He's just along for the ride."

"What would my mom think?" Troy asked.

"Your mom?" Troy's dad's eyebrows weighed heavy beneath a wrinkled forehead as he growled, "What's your mom got to do with us?"

"Dad, the last time I saw you, there were police helicopters in the air and you jumped off a bridge into the Chattahoochee."

Troy's father put on a sly grin. "The last time you saw me was on Lincoln Road."

"I knew it was you." Troy's face seemed to soften.

"And at the Atlanta zoo." Troy's dad kept grinning. "And when you were sitting outside on the patio at Wright's Gourmet Sandwich Shoppe. And after the championship game."

"I mean the last time I talked to you." Troy looked suddenly tired. "You're in trouble, Dad."

"And this"—Troy's father waved his hands around the room at the stuffed dead animals and their skins— "this is going to get me out of it! I won't have any trouble after this, Son. You *have* to help me. This is my *chance*."

"What are you talking about?" Troy's mouth fell open, and Ty froze.

"I'm talking about Super Bowl Sunday." Troy's father sat on the edge of his chair with his hands flat on the plank table as if he were ready to jump up out of his seat. "These people can fix everything for me. They're going to pay every debt, and I still get a million dollars on top of that! I can start over, Troy. Easy Street."

"The FBI wants you."

Troy's dad waved his hand again. "These people can give me a new identity. New Social Security number. Plastic surgery. Everything. The government isn't the only one who can hide people away."

"Why would they give you a million dollars? What are you talking about?"

"The game. The line is Falcons by seven. That's with you helping call the plays. Without you, they'll be lucky to win, let alone beat the point spread."

"Gambling?" Troy asked.

His father nodded. "Of course. This is the biggest event in gambling history. It's the Super Bowl! Without you, we know who wins."

"Without me?"

"Sure. That's all you have to do. Just sit here until Sunday night, you and your friend. Then you head right back to the hotel. You spent some time with your dad before he went away, and your friend here took a boat ride and got lost in the swamp. That's all. It's so simple. So perfect!"

Ty nodded. He was scared to death and just thankful that the plan included him being returned to his brother safely. He wanted to play in the championship and win the tournament on Sunday, but none of that mattered when you compared it to not being fed to the man-eaters and being set free.

"Well, that's not happening." Troy glared at his father with disgust and what might also have been hatred. Troy jumped up from his chair and headed for the door.

Troy's dad sprang, leaping over the table. Troy had his hand on the door handle when his father grabbed the collar of his shirt and yanked him back into a bear hug. Troy kicked and flailed, but his father was too strong and he carried him over to the couch, where he dumped him and stood towering over him. Troy sat straight and gripped the cushions beneath him.

Ty sat straight, too, and had to catch his breath.

Troy and his father were nose to nose, both of them glaring with flared nostrils, neither one backing down.

"My mother will know I'm gone." Troy spit out the words. "She'll look for me, and she'll find me."

A smile grew at the corners of his father's mouth.

"Your mother? Yeah, she'll look. That I know, but she ain't gonna find you. You want me to tell you why, smart guy? Because by now she already got a text message from your phone telling her you're with me in Miami and not to follow us. That's right, but they will follow us. It'll be an all-out manhunt for the NFL's football genius, and the police and the FBI will trace the cell tower the text was sent from and they'll see it came from downtown Miami. Yeah, Pete Bonito took a special trip down there just to send the message, and that's where they'll all look, everyone. The police, the FBI, and your mother, too."

An idea flashed into Ty's mind like a lightning bolt. He might be able to save himself and Troy, but he'd have only one chance and very little time to do it.

While Troy and his father stared each other down, Ty removed his bound hands from the tabletop and let his fingers fish for the cell phone in his pants pocket. He kept his eyes on the father and son as he slipped the phone free and held it in his lap, flipping it open. Ty's heart hammered the inside of his rib cage.

He glanced down and worked his thumbs to get into his contacts. He moved the cursor toward Thane's name and hit it, but missed Thane's and got Tate's, which was directly above Thane's.

"Hey!" Troy's dad was looking at Ty now and not his son. "What are you doing?"

CHAPTER SIXTY-ONE

TY'S THUMBS WORKED WITH lightning speed. He typed, "fishcamp," and just managed to hit *send* as Troy's dad snatched the phone from his hand, then pitched it against the far wall to shatter and drop among the feet of the stuffed animals on the floor. Ty winced at the sound of the smashing phone.

"What did you do?" Troy's dad demanded.

"Nothing." Ty looked the man straight in the eye. "I was just getting my phone."

"To do what? Call for help? You think that's smart? You do that and you'll ruin everything. You ruin everything, and I'm not going to be able to protect you from what Bonito and the Blade might do. You get it?"

Ty nodded.

"Good." Troy's dad turned his scowl back to Troy.

"Now, if you don't like it, if you don't want to help your own father, well I guess that's just the way you were raised. Pathetic if you ask me, but I can live with it. Either way, you and your buddy here aren't leaving this fish camp until Sunday, after the Super Bowl. That's final."

"You can't stop me." Troy glared. "You're going to have to tie me up like Ty. Is that what you're going to do? Is that how you treat your own son?"

Troy's father's face softened. "Let's not fight, Troy. This is the way it is. Even if I wanted to get out, you don't just get out with these people. We're in. Like it or not, we're in. You and me, and your friend."

Ty nodded, knowing it to be true, but neither father nor son saw him, and Ty wasn't about to tell them his story about the mob.

Troy didn't seem to be any happier about the situation. He folded his arms across his chest and stood up, then marched for the door again.

Troy's father took a deep breath before springing into action. He grabbed Troy and bent his arm behind his back in a chicken wing.

"Let's go," Troy's father said to Ty, motioning his head toward the rickety stairs in the corner. "You two aren't gonna play nice? Up."

Ty stood up from the table and started toward the stairs. Troy's father forced Troy that way too.

"That room right in front of you," Troy's dad said to

Ty when he reached the top landing.

Ty walked into the room. It had two small metal beds on either side, a single dresser, and two chairs. Green wool army blankets covered the sagging beds, and a striped pillow rested on each. A small door opened into a closet-sized bathroom, and two small windows looked out over the swamp. In the moonlight, Ty could see the dark water below. The shape of either a big log or a man-eating gator drifted by. Ty shuddered.

Troy's dad propelled Troy into the room. "You think about it up here for a bit. Get some sleep. In the morning, I'll see if you're ready to play nice. If you are, that Xbox and some cold pizza will be waiting for you. You might as well play nice, Troy. You're saving your father's life, whether you like it or not. I'd like to think you'll come to your senses. You think the Falcons *need* to win the Super Bowl? Why? For your mother's boyfriend? This is my *life* we're talking about. Think about that, because you better believe I'd do the same for you."

The door closed, and Ty heard the rattle of hardware before the unmistakable click of a padlock. Troy crossed the room and tried the door. It didn't budge.

"You can't do this!" Troy screamed through the door, pounding it with a fist.

CHAPTER SIXTY-TWO

WHEN TROY STOPPED POUNDING, he rested his arm against the door and buried his face. Ty heard a sniff and he looked away. Troy wiped his face on his arm and turned to face Ty.

"Let me get that off your wrists." Troy found the edge of the tape and picked at it. Once he got it started, the tape came off fast, sticking to Ty's skin as he yanked the last bit free.

"Ow."

"Sorry." Troy crumpled the tape into a ball and fired it at the wall before he looked up at Ty with red-rimmed eyes.

"It's okay, you gotta pull it off quick." Ty rubbed his wrists.

"I mean about everything," Troy said. "All this."

"It's not your fault."

"I never should have followed him. Why would I follow him?" Troy smacked the top of his own head.

"If I hadn't seen my dad in a long time and he just popped up and waved to me, I'd follow him, too," Ty said. "You didn't do anything wrong."

Troy looked at him. "I haven't even been nice to you."

"We're on different teams. That happens." Ty looked down at his shoes.

Troy crossed the room and eased open the old window; flecks of paint and dust filled the air. Troy looked down at the water and lowered his voice to a whisper. "Maybe we could jump. Swim for it."

Before Ty could point out the problem with that, Troy clenched his fists and shook his head at the water below. "Stupid. They'd eat us alive, those crazy things. We're trapped. There's no way out."

Ty cleared his throat. "There might be a way."

CHAPTER SIXTY-THREE

TROY AND TY PUT their chairs by the window so that they could watch for Tate to bring the police. They turned the bedroom light off to see better up the canal and into the gator pool and the mangroves beyond. Also, the light attracted moths, and they didn't want the room full of those. Outside, crickets and other insects sang, but not like a whole symphony the way they would sound in the summertime. This was more like a band of stragglers. It would have been peaceful and beautiful if they hadn't been kidnapped by two mobsters and Troy's crazy dad.

"You think she'll come?" Ty asked.

"If it was anyone else, I'd say I doubt it, but Tate? She'll be here. She'll know just what you meant when you said 'fishcamp.' I just hope she can convince the police that this is where we are and not in Miami. If they got my text when my dad said they did, they're probably already in gear and halfway downtown, if not there already."

"She wouldn't come by herself?"

Troy looked at him in the moonlight. "You don't know Tate."

As they sat watching, they could hear the sound of the Xbox below. From the sound of it, Troy's dad was battling an alien race of locusts in *Gears of War*.

"I can't even believe he's my dad," Troy said, staring out into the night. "For a lot of years, I actually ached to meet him and know who he was. Now, I think I wish he'd stayed in Chicago."

Ty didn't know what to say; finally he spoke. "You look a lot like him."

"My gramps says that's how come I'm a football player. My dad was too. My gramps thinks a lot of who we are is from our genes. I don't know. Maybe that's why I do things sometimes that aren't so great, like not being so nice to you. Maybe that's my father's part of me."

"My coach—not for the Seven-on-Seven, but my school coach—he said I'm a good receiver and fast like my brother. My brother says we got that from our mom. I guess she had a little brother who was a football player too, so football runs in both our families. I guess that's how my brother ended up in the NFL."

"My father would have been in the NFL, too," Troy said. "At least that's what my gramps said."

"What happened?"

"He broke his neck, I guess. He was a running back."

Ty sat up straight and put a hand on Troy's shoulder. "Not at . . . Alabama?"

Troy gave him a funny look. "How'd you know?"

"Your dad's name isn't Edinger, is it?"

"Did you read that in the paper?" Troy asked.

"Is it Edinger? Is it?"

"Yes."

"When I run fast, my brother says I look like an Edinger. My mom took second in the hundred meters at the NCAAs and she had a little brother who played running back at Alabama until he broke his neck. Troy, your dad is my mom's brother. You're my family. You're my cousin."

The smile on Troy's face bloomed slowly but surely.

"Cousins?" Troy said.

Ty nodded. "Tate even said we look kind of alike."

"That was partly why I think I wasn't so nice," Troy said. "She said that to me, too, and I hated it."

"We're cousins." Ty chuckled and hugged him. Troy hugged him back, laughing as well.

"This is crazy."

"This is great," Ty said, and then he froze. "What is that? A snake?"

Ty poked his head out the window. The hissing sound wasn't a snake. In the water below, sitting in the front seat of a two-person kayak, was Tate McGreer.

CHAPTER SIXTY-FOUR

TATE STOPPED HER HISSING but spoke in an urgent whisper. "Stop hugging each other and get down here."

Ty wanted to tell her they were cousins, but the seriousness of the situation came back to him, and he nodded before pulling his head back inside the window. "It's Tate. She's in a kayak."

"I told you," Troy said.

"How do we get down?"

Troy looked around the room. "Sheets."

"Sheets tied together? That's just in the movies."

Troy was already tearing the blankets off the bed. "I saw it on *MythBusters*. It really worked."

Ty watched as Troy tied the sheets together, then said, "Help me move the bed."

Together, they picked up the bed closest to the window

and quietly moved it so that the metal-framed head of the bed was right up next to the windowsill. Troy tied the sheet to the bed and tugged it tight. Troy whipped off his suit coat and tie and unbuttoned the collar of his white dress shirt before rolling up his sleeves. Ty did the same.

"Come on," Troy said to him, shoving the sheet out into the night before he backed out of the window.

Ty peered out and watched Troy lower himself down into the kayak. He had to hang above it for a moment while Tate positioned the second seat beneath him.

"There's no room," Ty said.

"I'll go in the middle." Troy climbed out of the seat and clung, lizardlike, to the top of the kayak between the two seats. The kayak wavered.

"I don't know," Tate said.

"We aren't leaving Ty behind."

"I know that," Tate said. "I thought we could fit two in a seat."

"No way. It's too small. Just come on. Hurry."

Ty turned around and backed out of the window, gripping the sheet ladder with all his strength and lowering himself down. He swung above the seat, wavering until Tate was able to back the kayak up underneath him. Ty's feet found the hole, and he lowered himself right down in. The paddle had been shoved in there too. Ty lifted it up, ready to go.

"How come you didn't bring help?" Troy asked Tate

in a hushed voice.

"I *tried*," Tate said. "You think I didn't try? I couldn't even get through to your mom's phone. It went right to voice mail, and I left a message. The stupid security guard at the hotel didn't even believe me. All he kept asking was where my parents were. I wasn't going to just sit around. I'm here, aren't I? So stop complaining and let's get going."

Tate pushed them off, using her paddle against one of the piers holding up the water side of the camp. Once they were out in the middle of the channel, she began to paddle them forward. Ty dug in too, careful not to splash. He turned his head and looked back at the cabin. The blue light of the TV flickered in the bottom window, and Ty could envision Troy's dad sitting there on the couch, fighting locusts, while they made their great escape. It made Ty giddy and he lost his balance, rocking the kayak a bit.

"Easy!" Troy said, his feet dipping into the water in an attempt to keep them from tipping.

"Sorry." Ty focused hard on his balance and on doing all he could to help propel them through the channel.

When they reached the large open pool where the man-eaters were, Ty swallowed and couldn't help glancing around. He shivered at the sight of Troy's left foot dipping into the dark water.

"Get your foot in," Ty said.

"I'm okay," Troy said. "Just get us out of here."

Ty worked hard and built up a sizable sweat by the time they reached the mangrove creek. Halfway through, he heard something slithering through the limbs above and knew it was a Burmese python. Ty dug in even harder, and in his excitement, banged a paddle blade against a mangrove root, sending a shock wave through the small tree and showering them with spider crabs.

Ty felt one scurry down his neck and into the open collar of his shirt. He lurched sideways, swatting at the disgusting crab. When he did, he heard two splashes.

The first was Troy dumping into the creek.

The second was the hungry python up ahead sensing easy prey in the water, and dropping in after it.

CHAPTER SIXTY-FIVE

TY SENSED THE BIG snake slithering through the water. Troy scrambled to get back up onto the narrow kayak, but the snake, flickering like a shadow even blacker than the water around it, was closing fast.

Ty raised his paddle up over his head and turned the blade. As soon as the snake got into range, he swung with all his might, connecting with the enormous reptile's head so that it writhed and slashed at the water around it.

Ty raised the paddle and swung again and again, pummeling the monster until it slithered off among the roots of the mangroves. Spider crabs skittered everywhere, along the top of the kayak and down in the hole where Ty sat. He didn't even care. He barely felt them as he caught his breath and helped lift Troy back into place.

Troy hugged the boat. "You saved me."

Ty couldn't even respond. He only paddled as Tate did, moving them toward the mouth of the creek and away from the deadly snake.

When they broke free from the mangroves, Ty let loose a jagged sigh and slumped forward in his seat, gripping Troy by the ankle and squeezing hard. "We made it."

They started down the channel that would take them to the final creek, a wider waterway without the overhang for spider crabs and snakes. They *had* made it.

"Nothing but open water between us and the hotel." Ty grinned.

That was when they heard the motor of a boat coming up the creek from the direction of the hotel.

"They're coming for us!" Tate said, practically shouting for joy. "It must be your brother and Troy's mom."

The three of them began to laugh as a swamp boat with a powerful spotlight emerged from the creek ahead and swung its beam full on them.

Ty rested his paddle across the boat and waved his hands like Tate and Troy. Their laughter lost itself in the whine of the boat's motor. The boat slowed as it pulled up alongside them. The light was too bright to see, but Ty's heart swelled at the sound of an adult voice.

"Hey, kids. Funny finding you out here."

Ty shielded his eyes from the spotlight, but that

wasn't necessary. The light snapped off, and the grins on the faces in the boat shone clear in the moonlight.

"I'd say our luck is holding out pretty well, Mr. Bonito."

"I'd say you're right on, Bennie."

CHAPTER SIXTY-SIX

TY LAY ON THE rough wooden floor, back in the upstairs bedroom, this time by himself and with no hope of getting free from Bennie the Blade's duct tape. Tate and Troy, he knew, were in the other two bedrooms on the second floor, and he presumed they, too, had been bound and gagged and secured to a metal bed so that there was no way they could move. If they even tried to move, it would raise a ruckus.

He strained to hear the voices downstairs, but they were too soft for him to understand.

Suddenly, the voices rose and Ty could just make out the words.

"You think we care what you think? You think you got a say in this? You're lucky we don't gut you and your kid, too." Ty shuddered at Pete Bonito's surly tone and knew the man meant business.

"You don't just kill kids." Troy's dad sounded more like a beggar than a person in control.

"*You* might not, but *we* got no choice." Bennie the Blade's voice had a soft, slippery quality to it, but his volume was equal to Bonito's. "We ain't gonna just disappear after this, Houdini. We got lives to live back in Jersey. We ain't having no witnesses."

"Your kid can go with you, but those other kids ain't leaving this swamp," Bonito said. "That's final."

There was a silent pause. Ty thought he might vomit and grew scared of choking on it before he realized it might be a better way to go than being gutted by Bennie the Blade's knife.

"Okay, you got me." Troy's dad broke the quiet. "I don't know why the heck I care. Hey, don't look at me like that, Bennie. Have a drink. Let's celebrate. This is going to be the biggest scam in the history of sports. Bigger than Pete Rose or Art Schlichster. Bigger than the BC basketball team. Heck, bigger than the Black Sox."

Laughter filled the room.

"Come on," Troy's dad said. "Let's have a drink."

"Let's have two!" Bonito said.

The men's voices became indistinct again, but Ty heard the clink of glasses as they toasted their success. The laughter continued, Troy's dad loudest of all. Ty closed his eyes and thought back to all the things he would miss. He would miss Thane most of all. He would miss knowing his cousin Troy and maybe even getting to see Tate on a regular basis. He would miss the two of them connecting for Halpern Middle, or maybe even playing for Don Bosco, the New Jersey high-school football powerhouse. He'd miss the smell of the grass, stepping out onto the field in the 7-on-7 championship game on Super Bowl Sunday. He'd miss a lot of things, and he was terrified because he knew this was it.

The only consolation was that it would soon be over. He could stop being afraid all the time, and he'd finally be with his parents. Ty shut his eyes as tight as they would go and prayed to God there was a heaven and that he really could be with his mom and dad. But he was afraid of even that. Afraid heaven wasn't true. Afraid God was just words. He didn't think that, but he couldn't help being afraid.

That was how he lay, barely aware of the noise below him, overwhelmed by his fear and squirming in torment from his duct tape bonds as well as the thought of his certain death. Ty didn't know how much time had passed before he realized that it had gone quiet again downstairs, but it had. Another eternity seemed to pass before he heard the soft creak of footsteps on the stairs. Slowly they came, and with them Ty's belly filled with poisonous dread, absolute horror.

The door creaked as it swung open. Ty's eyes widened in terror as the shadow of a man slipped inside.

The slick sound of a blade slipping free from its sheath was followed by the glint of that metal weapon as it caught the moonlight spilling in through the window.

Ty could hear the man's heavy breathing as he knelt above him, blocking out the moonlight but not the glow of the long knife blade.

Ty's body bucked uncontrollably, fighting the bonds of tape. He squeezed his eyes shut tight, spilling hysterical tears down his cheeks. A sobbing groan filled the cavity behind his nose as he felt the unmistakable chill of the blade against his skin.

Ty knew he was about to die.

CHAPTER SIXTY-SEVEN

"SH."

The sound whispered in Ty's ear confused him, even as he heard the slicing sound of the blade.

"Sh."

Nothing hurt, and Ty wondered if that was why desperate people sometimes cut their wrists, because it didn't really hurt. In fact, Ty felt nothing at all until the pressure of his duct tape handcuffs was released. He flexed his hands and grasped for the floor as if the whole building tilted beneath him.

He blinked as the dark figure bent now to his feet, cutting them free as well. Ty's hands went to his mouth to remove the tape, but the hand without the knife held him at bay. The man shook his head no, and Ty saw now that it was Troy's father.

Troy's father held a finger to his lips, signaling complete silence. Then he removed the finger from his lips and signaled for Ty to stay still. Ty rubbed the feeling back into his wrists and ankles as he sat on the floor, waiting. Troy's dad wasn't gone long before he returned with Troy and Tate in tow, both of them moving awkwardly as they, too, tried to regain the feeling in their hands and feet. Their mouths also remained taped shut, and Ty realized it was to ensure everyone's silence.

"Okay." Troy's father spoke in the faintest of whispers. "Let's go."

Troy turned toward the stairs, but his father stopped him, shaking his head and pointing to the window. Troy's father eased it open and whispered, "I'll go first. You climb down my back. Hang on to my collar, then my belt, and then my feet. It'll work."

Ty and Troy looked out the window. The swamp boat had been tied to a pier.

The sheet ladder had been disposed of by Pete Bonito before, while Bennie the Blade taped Ty up, but now Troy's father would be their ladder. The big man climbed out the window and clung to its ledge with thick, bony fingers. Tate went first, scrambling down his back and into the boat. Ty went next, dropping into the bottom of the boat and looking up at Troy's dad as he hung like a man clinging to a burning building. Troy came out and started down.

His father's arms began to shake, and one hand

slipped from its grip on the window. Troy fell the final eight feet and collapsed into the bottom of the boat with a snap.

A low, painful sound bubbled up from Troy's gut as he grasped his ankle. Ty helped him out of the way, and Troy's dad dropped down, too, landing more skillfully with a thump and a groan.

Instead of starting the motor, Troy's dad removed an oar from beneath the seats. He untied the boat from the pier and slowly paddled them down the channel. Not until his father had paddled them across the man-eater pool and into the creek did he bend over and yank the motor to life. When he did, he stayed heavy on the throttle, telling them all it was safe to remove the tape from their mouths. All three of them carefully peeled back the tape as they surged through the mangrove creek and out into the next channel, racing north and swishing into the second creek.

They hit the open canal, and the boat motor whined ever louder. The hotel rose up above the trees, a beacon in the night, shining bright and white and growing ever taller, as if it were rising up out of the earth. When they broke into the body of water behind the hotel, Ty looked back over his shoulder, past Troy's dad, past the foamy wake of water, half expecting to see the mobsters hot on their trail.

All Ty saw was the moon, the water, and the dark shadows of the trees.

They had made it.

Troy's dad pulled in to the marina and helped them up onto the deck. Light from the VIP party glowed above the gardens, and music thumped the night air. Troy had to be lifted up and left to sit on the dock's edge because he could put no weight on his ankle. His dad stepped back in the boat and looked up at them all, smiling awkwardly.

"This ought to take care of us winning the Seven-on-Seven championship." Troy's voice was less bitter than Ty would have expected.

Troy's dad held out a hand, and Troy shook it before letting his dad pull him into a tight hug.

"I'm sorry, Troy."

Troy let him go and shook his head, obviously not even knowing what to say.

"Thanks." Ty startled himself by breaking the silence.

"Yeah, thanks. You saved us, Mr. Edinger," Tate said.

Troy's dad nodded. "I never thought in a million years you two kids would get involved or those nutcases would start talking about killing people. It was all business to me. It was a great shot to make a ton of money and dig myself out of this hole. I hope you know that."

"We know," Tate said.

Troy's dad scratched his head, then reached out and gave Troy's shoulder a squeeze. He laughed in a lighthearted way, even though his face was sad. "Well, gotta go."

Troy's dad pressed his lips tight and gave one final nod before firing up the swamp boat. They stood watching as the Everglades swallowed him up and even the sound of the motor was gone.

"What do you think will happen to him?" Tate asked.

"I hope he'll be all right," Ty said. "Those people are pretty bad and they're not gonna be happy when they wake up."

Troy kept staring out at the big swamp and he sighed. "He'll be all right. He always is."

CHAPTER SIXTY-EIGHT

THE GEORGIA TEAM DIDN'T give up, and neither did Troy.

Ty's cousin stood on crutches beside his coach, feeding his teammates information, sometimes even shouting out to them the play that was about to be run. Somehow it didn't seem fair to Ty, but Coach Bavaro scoffed at that on the Raptors' sideline.

"That kid is just doing what we do with our film study and hours and hours of meetings," Coach Bavaro told his team. "He just does it in a split second. I'd do the same thing if I were them, so you guys stop complaining and let's beat them anyway."

That had been early in the game, and now "beating them anyway" wasn't looking good. There were only five seconds left. The Raptors had used their final time-out and the ball rested on the forty-yard line.

There was time for one last play. Ty looked over at Troy White, who studied the Raptors with a calm eye from the Georgia sideline. Beyond him sat a crowd of several thousand people, not enough to make a place like the Dolphins' stadium look even close to full, but enough to add noise to the excitement of playing in a championship on ESPN 2.

David Bavaro took the signal from his father on the sideline and called the play.

"Wait!" Ty said.

Everyone froze.

"Let's not run that play."

"My dad called it," David Bavaro said. "He's the coach."

"Let's *almost* run it." Ty's voice sounded confident, even to himself.

"Almost?"

"Strahan, don't run the corner route." Ty felt in command. "That's what they'll expect from that formation and in this situation. Run a comeback instead. Even Troy White won't guess that's coming."

"He won't guess it's coming because why would Strahan run a comeback?" Bavaro said. "It's the last play. We need to get into the end zone."

"But if they know it's coming, they'll defend against it," Ty said. "He can run the comeback, and I'll do an out-and-up right behind him. Michael, catch the ball, and pitch it back to me."

"Hook and lateral?" Strahan said, the gap in his teeth showing with his smile. "We never ran that before."

"Exactly," Ty said. "We never ran it. *He's* never seen it. He can't predict something that's not even in our playbook, right?"

"Maybe he can." Bavaro looked doubtful.

"Pitch it to me and I can race right up the sideline and into the end zone," Ty said. "Come on. What have we got to lose?"

Everyone agreed and David Bavaro nodded, repeating what everyone would do before breaking the huddle. Ty lined up inside of Michael Strahan Jr. at the slot position. He kept his eyes ahead, afraid that Troy could somehow read his mind. The ball was snapped and Ty took off.

Strahan broke off his route and caught the ball. Ty cut out, then surged up the sideline with blazing speed. As the defenders closed on Strahan, he flicked the ball to Ty, and two seconds later Ty held the ball high in the end zone.

His team mobbed him, whooping and hollering and laughing out loud.

When the craziness settled, they lined up and shook hands with the team from Georgia. Ty and Troy brought up the back of each of their lines, working their way through until they found themselves standing together on the Georgia sideline. Troy leaned on his crutches to free a hand so he could shake with Ty. Tate ran up to them both.

She patted Troy on the back. "Sorry, Troy."

"It's okay. That's the game."

Tate turned to Ty, beaming. "Congratulations, Ty. You were incredible."

Ty felt his cheeks burning. He couldn't speak, only shake his head.

"How'd you do that, anyway?" Troy asked. "You never ran that play before. I can't believe your coach called that. He never calls plays he doesn't practice."

"How do you know?" Ty asked.

Troy shrugged. "I can't really explain it."

"It's like the weather; he just gets a feeling," Tate said.

"I made it up," Ty said.

"You?"

"In the huddle."

Troy grinned. "Don't you tell a soul."

"I won't. I'm rooting for the Falcons tomorrow, and then after that, it's J-E-T-S, Jets, Jets, Jets."

Troy laughed and Ty did too, then they hugged each other.

"I'll see you in New Jersey, Cousin."

"I can show you around," Ty said. "Both of you."

Troy and Tate looked at each other. "We're counting on it."

"You'll come see me—us?" Ty asked Tate.

"Of course." She tucked a loose end of hair behind her ear. "You couldn't get rid of me in an endless swamp, you think I won't find you in New Jersey?"

Ty hugged her too, then jogged back across the field.

When Ty returned to his bench, Thane was waiting there with a surprise.

"Agent Sutherland?" Ty said, not sure if the man with blond hair was really the agent in disguise or just a twin with hair.

"He came to apologize," Thane said. "They got it wrong, again."

Sutherland's face went red. He took off his sunglasses and nodded. "We had the wrong guy."

"What do you mean?"

Sutherland sighed and said, "I couldn't tell you the truth because we didn't want to compromise the operation, but we knew they were down here. We thought it was your brother they wanted, so we tracked every move he made."

"Tracked my brother? On the beach?"

Sutherland nodded. "I almost lost my pension for that one."

"That was you?"

Sutherland nodded and replaced his sunglasses. "All's well that ends well, though. We nabbed them this morning. I wanted to tell you personally. They've all got prior felonies. They'll go away forever with this kidnapping charge."

"Troy's dad, too?" Ty asked.

Sutherland shook his head. "Him we didn't get, but we will. He's not the dangerous one, though. You got nothing to worry about, Ty. It's over for Bennie and Bonito."

Ty's heart began to soar, but then it came back down. "But didn't you say that they're like roaches? Squash one and there's always another to take his place?"

Sutherland nodded. "That's true, except this thing could bring the whole house down. Word on the street is that the D'Amico family bet everything they've got on tonight's game. If the Falcons win and cover the spread, the D'Amico organization will not only lose everything they have, they'll owe the other families a ton of money, and that won't go over well."

"So, they're not going to have time to worry about me or Ty or even Uncle Gus," Thane said.

"No. Their problems will be a lot more serious than you folks."

When Ty spoke, it was almost to himself. "I never thought I'd root so hard for a team to win the Super Bowl."

And so, when Troy helped the Falcons win it that night by a score of 31–10, Ty felt like someone had truly and finally set him free.

EXTRAS

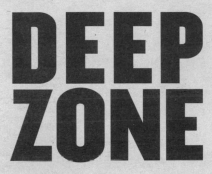

DEEP ZONE

Q&A with Tim Green

Fast Facts about the Super Bowl

A Sneak Peek at *Unstoppable*

Q&A with Tim Green

1) Thane is worried that his leg injury might be permanent and he won't be able to play in the NFL. What advice would you give young players to avoid injury and stay healthy during football season?

The most important thing you can do to stay healthy during football season is maintain a rigorous strength training program in the off-season. You want to do as much as you can to build up your strength through lifting weights and other exercises your coach suggests, so that you're in the best possible shape when practice starts. If a player does get injured, he should never make the decision himself about whether to try to play through it or not. The player should always go to the coach, the trainer, or even the team doctor, if there is one, and a good coach is going to send the player to the trainer or the doctor anyway. Instead of playing with too much pain and making the injury worse, the player should let the trainer make the decision.

2) Thane tells Ty that school always comes before football. Why is school so important even for star athletes?

I always tell kids that to be a professional athlete, you need talent and hard work, but also—on top of all that—a tremendous amount of luck. You can give it everything you have and still not make it to the pros. But whatever energy you put into your school work will always pay you back. The work you put into school to become a doctor, a teacher, a lawyer, an engineer, or whatever you want to be—that work will pay you back. You don't need to be lucky to be any of those things. You just need to work hard.

3) Is the Seven-on-Seven Super Bowl tournament based on a real competition?

Seven-on-Seven tournaments are real, and they're increasingly popular, but this particular tournament at the Super Bowl, sponsored by the NFL, is my invention based on the quickly growing popularity of the actual tournaments. There is no one official league for these tournaments—different places have their own separate leagues. But they're usually not affiliated with schools. Seven-on-Seven tournaments have become a proving ground for the football players and coaches to work on and show off their passing games, because there are no line men. If you're interested in playing on a Seven-on-Seven team, you should talk to your football coach to see if there's a league nearby during the off-season. Or you can find one online.

4) When Ty uses Facebook to get in contact with his cousin Charlotte, the FBI warns him that the communication can be traced. Do you have any advice for aspiring young athletes about online profiles and internet privacy?

Certainly. Everyone needs to understand the importance of keeping personal information offline, and that includes future athletes. Maybe you are so comfortable with Facebook and with the internet that you feel like you have some level of privacy, but in reality you don't. It's important to understand that anything you put on Facebook is going to be there for everyone to see forever. It's easily accessible by coaches and other important people. The mistakes you make online as a kid could stick with you for the rest of your life. You're no longer relying on people's memories of something you did—it will be up online forever. So think twice and be very careful about what you decide to post.

5) Ty's team watches a lot of film coverage during the Seven-on-Seven tournament. What do you look for when watching films of an opponent, and how much of an advantage does this give a team?

First of all, any film work needs to be led by a coach or someone who has a pretty advanced understanding of the game and strategy. A young football player shouldn't expect to be able to look at film of an opponent and be able to figure significant things out.

It takes years to be proficient in it, and you need the tutelage of a good coach to figure out how to do it. Once you do have the expertise, though, watching film of previous games is a great way of showing players what's going to happen on the field next time, before it happens. You can tell when your opponents get in a certain formation, it means they're probably going to run this or that play. And that gives you a huge advantage.

6) Did you always know Troy and Ty were going to be cousins when you were writing *Football Genius* and *Football Hero*?
I knew from the beginning that they were going to be cousins. When I was writing *Football Hero*, which introduces Ty, I built the connection into that book. They've always looked similar, and that's why. I knew I would one day write a book that would bring these two characters together, although I wasn't sure what that book would look like. I didn't know until I started writing *Deep Zone* that they would meet up during the Super Bowl.

Fast Facts about the Super Bowl*

- The Super Bowl started as part of a merger between the National Football League (NFL) and the American Football League (AFL). Now, each of these two leagues is called a "conference" within the NFL, and the two conference champions play in the Super Bowl during the first week of February.
- The first Super Bowl was held in Memorial Coliseum in Los Angeles in 1967. The Green Bay Packers defeated the Kansas City Chiefs, 35–10.
- The Pittsburgh Steelers and the Dallas Cowboys have each played in eight Super Bowls. The Steelers have the NFL record for most wins with six. Sixteen other teams have won at least one Super Bowl. Ten teams have appeared in the Super Bowl without a win.
- The Super Bowl is frequently the most watched American television broadcast of the year.
- The team that wins the Super Bowl receives the Vince Lombardi Trophy, named after the former coach of the Green Bay Packers. The Packers won the first two Super Bowl games in 1967 and 1968.
- Over half of the Super Bowl games so far have been played in just three cities: New Orleans (nine times), the Greater Miami area (ten times), and the Greater Los Angeles area (seven times). The 2012 Super Bowl was held at the Lucas Oil Stadium in Indianapolis, Indiana.
- No team has ever played the Super Bowl in its own home stadium.
- The location of the Super Bowl is chosen by the NFL well in advance, usually four years before the game is even played!
- One team is designated as the "home team" and one team is designated as the "away team." The AFC team is the home

---

* All Fast Fact statistics were compiled following Super Bowl XLVI in 2012.

team during even-numbered games and the NFC team is the home team during odd-numbered games.

- Away teams have won more than half of the Super Bowl games to date—twenty-six of forty-six.
- The Super Bowl Most Valuable Player (MVP) award is presented at the end of every Super Bowl game to a single player who is voted on by fans, sports writers, and broadcasters.
- Joe Montana is the only player to have won three Super Bowl MVP awards, but four other players have won the award twice: Bart Starr, Terry Bradshaw, Tom Brady, and Eli Manning.

UNSTOPPABLE

CHAPTER ONE

HARRISON ADMIRED THE NFL football player, battered and exhausted but unstoppable. Harrison knew about being battered and exhausted, not by the game, but by life. The player looked like a gladiator. Harrison looked like an overgrown farm kid. The player wore a green uniform with silver eagles' heads on the sleeves. Harrison looked down at his own stained and dirty coveralls and the worn-down boots poking from beneath tattered cuffs.

Sweat matted the player's long blond hair and beard. Blood ran down his face, but a light still shone in his eyes. Ghosts of steam curled up from his bare arms in the chilly night air. Skin slick with sweat stretched tight over bulging muscles. The crowd roared its cheers, urging the player and his teammates on to deeds of greatness. Harrison ached to be a football player and for people to cheer him on, but he never could, and they never would. Every day when the final school bell rang, instead of joining the other boys for football practice, Harrison hurried home for chores.

The player on the big-screen TV rammed a helmet down on his head, and the camera followed him out onto the field where he crouched, waiting. When the other team ran a sweep to the outside, the player swooped in like a real eagle, striking the runner, hitting him low and lifting him into the air so that he flipped and crashed to the turf. The player flexed his bare arms and stomped across the field in a parade of glory. The crowd went wild and Harrison couldn't keep still. A small, satisfied grunt escaped his lips.

Mr. Constable pounded his beer can onto the coffee table, spun around on the couch, and glared. "What are you doin' here, Mud?"

Harrison stepped back into the shadow of the doorway. Mr. Constable had called him "Mud" since the day he arrived. That didn't keep Harrison from continuing to think of himself as Harrison, and he threatened the two younger kids, Flossy and Crab, into calling him Harrison in private, even though Dora and Lump, the two older kids, called him Mud.

"I said 'what'?"

Harrison jumped and knew to answer. "Watching."

"You got chores. You don't watch." Mr. Constable raised a fist to prove it. The other hand crept toward his belt.

Harrison nodded, retreating toward the front door of

the old farmhouse. Mrs. Constable appeared at the top of the stairs, her hair pulled so tight against her head that her forehead shined like a clean dinner plate. She puckered her lips and shook her head in disgust.

"Shoo!" she said, as if he were a big rodent.

Harrison returned to the barn and found his rusted shovel leaning in the doorway. A single bulb swung from the rafters, pushed by a small breeze. A cow shifted in one of the sick stalls. Her hooves scratched the dry hay. With the shovel in hand, Harrison dropped down into the milking parlor and the soup of manure. Green, brown, yellow—it depended on the feed the cows had taken. Harrison remembered the first time he'd smelled it, and the taste of vomit in the back of his throat.

Shadows flickered in the back corner of the parlor, and Harrison heard the hiss of hoses as Dora and Lump sprayed down the last of the milking machines. He began to shovel, slowly working the soup into the concrete channel and then down the channel until it disappeared into the night, plopping into the spreader below with a sloppy sound Harrison could sometimes hear in his sleep. The smell of cigarette smoke brought with it Cyrus Radford. The orange ember on the tip of the cigarette glowed in the doorway like the single eye of an angry little goblin before Cyrus stepped into the light.

"Where you been, Mud?" Cyrus wore coveralls like Harrison, also spattered with manure, but with no T-shirt underneath to cover the leathery skin draped over his raggedy bones. He scratched the gray-and-black stubble on his chin and spit on the floor.

"Mr. Constable called me into the house." Harrison didn't like to lie, but it was better than a beating.

He knew Cyrus wouldn't question him being called into the house by Mr. Constable. Even though Harrison suspected that Cyrus hated Mr. Constable as much as any of the kids, Cyrus would never show it. Cyrus was afraid of Mr. Constable just like the rest of them. Who wouldn't be? Mr. Constable was a giant, thick and strong and rumbling with anger at everything life put down before him. His blond hair had begun to fade, but his face was as red as a baby's. His blue eyes were so pale, they sometimes seemed to glint back at Harrison like mirrors, making Mr. Constable seem something more, or less, than human.

"Well, finish up." Cyrus raised an arm to scratch at the hair in its naked pit. "It's late and I need a drink."

Cyrus Radford lived alone in a trailer resting on cinder blocks down by the main road. He supervised the milking at five in the morning, noon, and eight o'clock at night. Dora—who was sixteen—and Lump—fifteen—had the job of slipping the suction cups onto the cows' udders as they crowded into the milking parlor. Only Cyrus was allowed to remove the milking machines because Mr. Constable didn't trust any of his kids to know when the cow was completely empty. Harrison's job was to keep the barn clean, an unending and impossible task in a world of manure, dirt, and flies.

The younger kids helped Mrs. Constable around the house, and Harrison didn't envy them, because even though his job was dirtier and smellier, the younger kids were much closer to the tattered end of Mr. Constable's belt. Mr. Constable believed in his belt, just as he believed children needed hard work in order to improve. As the foster father of dozens of kids over the years, Mr. Constable said that was his mission in life, to improve wayward young people in order for the world to be a better place.

Harrison shoveled harder, trying to make up for the time he'd spent watching *Monday Night Football* from the doorway, scraping the concrete and spattering the manure so that tiny droplets speckled his face. Sweat dripped from his nose, and his older foster siblings had already disappeared when he heard Mr. Constable cough from the barn door. Harrison shoveled double-time, scraping and scratching and spattering, because he had a bad feeling about Mr. Constable's huge frame filling the doorway.

"Mud!"

Harrison looked up. Cyrus bobbed behind Mr. Constable—just beyond the lightbulb's reach.

"Yes, sir?"

"You been lyin', boy. You been lyin', again."

Mr. Constable removed the belt and flicked it against the concrete floor with a snap.

CHAPTER TWO

CYRUS DANCED A JIG behind Mr. Constable. Cyrus always liked to watch when Mr. Constable went to work. Cyrus did his share of beating the kids, but he didn't seem to delight in it the way he did when Mr. Constable used the belt. Maybe because Cyrus's switch didn't leave the deep, dark bruises that followed the lick of a belt.

"Ain't you?" Mr. Constable flicked the belt in the air with another expert snap.

Harrison nodded. Tears welled up in his eyes, but they weren't tears from fear; they were tears of rage. He didn't deserve the belt for sneaking a peek at the football game. He did his work, harder than the rest. He could lift two bales of hay at the same time and toss them up onto the back of a truck like they were sacks of groceries. So the fact that he would feel the sting of the belt made him want to explode. His fists clenched, and for the first time in the thirteen long years of his life, he thought about using them against an adult.

He had used his fists against other kids, plenty. That's what landed him at the Constables' home in the first place. It was the fourth foster home he'd been passed on to—passed on for fighting with other children. But it wasn't the kind of fighting people thought it was. Harrison fought for survival. Sometimes he even fought for others, kids weaker and more frightened than him of the older kids who seemed to haunt their lives.

At his last home Harrison had bloodied the noses and blackened the eyes of two boys three years older than him. No one seemed to care that those same two boys had forced a little kid named Wally to lie down in the grass so they could pee on him. No one seemed to listen, only talk in quiet, hard voices about Harrison, comparing him to a zoo animal, an untamed and untamable beast. That's why he had landed with the Constables. Mr. Constable was known throughout the county as a foster father who could cure even the hardest of bargains. Harrison now knew why.

CRACK!

Harrison turned and looked to the opening at the other end of the barn, but where would he run? He'd run before and knew that it only led to hunger, cold, and ultimately a ride home in the back of a police car before someone "whipped some sense into you."

"Don't you even look at me like that, boy. Mud boy. You came from mud and you'll return to mud. That's how I named you. Don't be flashin' those angry eyes at *me*. I'll put the lights right out of 'em."

Harrison let his shoulders sag.

"That's better. Say you're sorry to Mr. Radford here."

Cyrus held still and wore the blank look of disappointment. An apology had absolutely no entertainment value for Cyrus.

"I'm sorry, Cy—Mr. Radford."

"That's better." Mr. Constable threaded the belt back into his pants. "And you can thank your lucky stars we got to see the judge tomorrow; otherwise I'd be tanning your sorry hide. Don't you think I gone soft."

"The judge, sir?" Harrison tried to keep the hope from seeping into his voice. Mr. Constable didn't like the sound of hope.

"Just got a call from the lawyer. Seems your momma's got some funny notions again. Raised a ruckus at the county offices on Friday. Won't come to nothin'. Never do. Finish up. Take a bath so you don't smell for the judge. Then get to bed. I won't even ask you to stop lying. It's just in your nature." Mr. Constable turned and shuffled off into the darkness.

Cyrus checked over his shoulder before he stepped into the barn, picked his own willow switch from its place on the wall, and smacked it against Harrison's rump. Harrison spun with his fists clenched again. The grin on Cyrus's face went out.

"That's the last time." The words came out of Harrison's mouth without him even thinking. "You do that again and I'll be on you like stink on a cow patty."

Cyrus's mouth fell open and he pointed the switch at Harrison. "You get back to work before I tell Mr. Constable what you're up to. You think you're gettin' outta here from some judge? Your momma's a tramp and a druggie. She cast you off like garbage, and once a woman does that there ain't a judge in creation hands her back her kids, so don't you get so smart."

Harrison stared at Cyrus for a minute, until the older man blinked; then Harrison took up his shovel and got back to work. His hands shook as he shoveled and replayed the scene that had just occurred over in his mind. He looked at his own arms, the thick cords of muscles, hard from work. His feet bulged out the sides of boots made for a full-grown man, and he realized that something had tilted the balance. He had been ready to fight Cyrus, not because he thought he'd get free, but because he thought he could win. At thirteen, he was as big and fast and strong as a weak man. Stronger, in fact, than a man as weak and meanspirited as Cyrus, and he knew in his heart that one part of the nightmare was over. A grim smile twisted his lips.

Harrison finished his work and shut out the light. A cow brayed at him from the herd that shifted and stamped quietly in their pen as he crossed the yard.

"Shush," Harrison said, still trembling at the exciting realization about Cyrus.

In the bath, he took special care to scrub beneath his nails, behind his ears, and between his toes. He didn't want to look or smell like a farm boy tomorrow. He would see the judge. He might even see his own mother. Cyrus's cruel words about her came back to him and his ears burned with shame and hate. Maybe that was why he had been ready to fight.

He lay down on the bed between his brothers: Lump, a boy who'd once been known as Michael, and Crab, who called himself Luke, until the belt won out. Sleep came hard for Harrison. Tomorrow was apt to be like every other day in his life, disappointing and hopeless. Yet, something told him that it might not.

It just might not.

CHAPTER THREE

MRS. CONSTABLE BOUGHT CORNFLAKES in plastic bins the size of garbage cans. She had an old coffee cup on a string that she used to serve out a full scoop to each of the kids every morning for breakfast. And, despite the fact that the farm produced fresh milk every day, Mrs. Constable filled her kids with the powdered milk she got for free from the county. Harrison hated that soapy-tasting pale blue liquid, but he was hungry enough that he'd eat it on his cereal without a word of complaint, and he supposed that the words Mrs. Constable sometimes muttered to herself were true.

"Don't need to waste good milk on kids like these."

After breakfast, Mrs. Constable sent him back upstairs to wash behind his ears again. When he returned, she took her scissors out of the sewing drawer and told him to sit still on the kitchen stool so she could cut a straight line around his head just below the ears. Harrison did his best not to move, but still Mrs. Constable managed to nick an ear. She handed him a paper towel to stop the blood, and Harrison tried to whisk the tiny pieces of cut hair free from his neck, where they'd settled into the collar of his only white button-down dress shirt.

Mr. Constable appeared in his work clothes, ordered half a dozen fried eggs from his wife, and disappeared up the stairs to change into his brown suit. As Harrison cleaned up the mess from his haircut, he couldn't help sniffing the air as the eggs crackled in their puddles of butter. He knew if he was sly enough, he'd get to lick Mr. Constable's plate before it made its way into the sink for cleaning. Harrison laid his plans as he swept the kitchen floor. By working slow, he was able to delay long enough that he could fill Mr. Constable's coffee cup, then clean out the grinds from the pot, working slowly again, and offering to clean up the table.

"Don't you mess that shirt." Mrs. Constable glared over the tops of her glasses, and Harrison wondered how just the thought of a dirty shirt could make someone so angry.

"I won't. You want me to clean the dishes too, ma'am?"

"The boy doesn't run from work, I'll say that." Mrs. Constable sniffed with pleasure. Even though she had a dishwasher, Mrs. Constable complained about the electricity it used and preferred one of the kids do them by hand.

"If he weren't such a godforsaken liar, he'd almost be worth somethin'." Mr. Constable jammed a piece of buttered toast into his mouth and chewed from side to side like one of his own cows.

Harrison made his move on the plate, removing it from the checkered tablecloth and hurrying to the sink, where he got in two quick licks before slipping it into the soapy water.

"Did you lick that plate?" Mrs. Constable's voice cut his ears like a razor.

"No, ma'am," Harrison lied without pause.

"You better *not*." Mrs. Constable removed the plate from the soap and smudged at it with her fingertip.

Harrison didn't ask why she cared whether the soapy water got the dribs of yolk instead of him. "No, ma'am."

After the scrape of his chair, Mr. Constable stood and belched and pulled on his suit coat. "Time. I'll be back, Mrs."

"You call him 'Papa,' you hear?" Mrs. Constable dropped the plate into the water and scowled. "That's how you address Mr. Constable with the judge. You forget that and I'll have a bar of soap to feed you before afternoon chores."

Harrison knew well the taste of laundry soap, and he had to admit that it was a good reminder to call Mr.

Constable "Papa." Harrison climbed into the bed of the pickup truck with Zip, the jug-headed yellow Lab. The truck jounced down the driveway, jarring Harrison's bones until the tires hummed on the smooth blacktop. The wind whisked through his shortened hair and Harrison flicked at the tiny brown pieces still clinging to his neck. Town held the county courthouse and several brick government buildings as well as the crumbling storefronts of the past hundred and fifty years. Once busy with trade from the railroad, they now sold nothing much more than yarn and used furniture. There were also two bars, a diner, and a nail shop, while the rest of the windows held FOR SALE signs behind their dusty glass.

The courthouse was a busy place, though. Just outside town a large modern prison housed the state's less dangerous criminals and offered up most of the good jobs for fifty miles around. Half the people in the courthouse seemed to be prisoners, and none of them was ever as glum as Harrison would be if he had to wear handcuffs and an orange jumpsuit. Mr. Constable's shoes clapped against the wood floor after they passed through a metal detector, and Harrison followed him to the back part of the courthouse, the new part with low ceilings, fake blond wood, and fluorescent tubes of light.

In a courtroom that looked more like a classroom to Harrison, the judge sat on a low platform behind his bench. A state flag drooped alongside the American flag, and a brass clock hung on the wall. Mr. Constable waved to the lawyer, and they sat down. Harrison scanned the room for his mother, but she wasn't to be seen. The judge scolded two teenage boys in orange jumpsuits before banging his gavel on the desk and watching them be ushered out by an armed guard. The boys looked scared, and the judge seemed satisfied with that.

Harrison tugged at the collar of his shirt, replaying all the things he'd done recently that might put him in the company of the imprisoned boys.

"Harrison Johnson."

The bailiff looked out over the courtroom. Mr. Constable leaned close. "Don't forget—'Papa.'"

Mr. Constable stood. Harrison did too, and followed his foster father to the front along with the lawyer, a greasy-looking man in a green suit with food stains on its sleeves.

"Melinda Johnson?" The bailiff craned his neck and Harrison turned his head, also scanning the room. "Ms. Johnson? Melinda Johnson?"

Mr. Constable spoke to the lawyer under his breath. "All this fuss and she's too drunk to show up."

The lawyer nodded as if it was just another expected part of his job.

Harrison's heart sank.

"Is Melinda Johnson here, or counsel for Ms. Johnson?" The judge looked up over the top of his glasses and glared out across the room, clenching his teeth until the cords pulsed in his neck. "I see. Mr. Constable, will you approach the bench with your ward and counsel, please?"

The judge looked at Harrison with distaste before turning his attention to the lawyer. "Mr. Denny, do you have the paperwork for this boy's adoption?"

The lawyer fumbled with his briefcase, nodding and winking until he came up with a thick packet of papers. "Right here, your honor."

"Then," the judge said, examining the papers, "given the trouble Ms. Johnson has caused in all this and her apparent lack of responsibility—as well as respect for this court, I might add—all leads me to believe that the best course of action for this young . . . boy is to make him the legal and permanent son of Mr. and Mrs. Brad Constable."

A look passed between Mr. Constable and the lawyer that Harrison didn't like. It was the look of two bank robbers who'd been invited into the vault. Harrison scanned the courtroom behind him again, feeling desperate and sensing that something very big was about to happen, something that would change the course of his life.

Something that couldn't be put right again.

Something very bad.

CHAPTER FOUR

MR. CONSTABLE TOOK AN oath.

The teeth in his big head had too much room between them to form a complete smile, but it was the closest thing Harrison could remember to one. At the clerk's desk, the grown-ups signed papers while Harrison stood in his stiff white shirt, the hair itching him to no end. Panic choked him and he was unable to voice the protest he felt certain he should be making.

Mr. Constable nudged him before Harrison realized they were all staring at him and waiting for him to speak.

"Isn't that right, Son?" Mr. Constable asked.

"Yes, sir."

Mr. Constable's smile tightened and his eyes seemed to radiate heat. "You don't have to call me that, Son.

Call me what you always call me."

"Yes . . . Papa."

For some unknown reason, that made the adults chuckle. The judge took the papers the lawyer handed to him, added his own signature, pronounced Harrison Johnson officially and legally to be Harrison Constable, and struck the desk with his mallet.

There was a ruckus at the back of the courtroom as someone forced open the doors with a shriek.

CHAPTER FIVE

HARRISON FELT HIS INSIDES melt like butter in a hot pan.

His mother's dark frizzy hair shot out from her head in all directions. She wore a long raincoat and Harrison didn't know what else besides a dirty pair of fluffy pink slippers. He could see the red in her eyes from across the room and the heavy bags of exhaustion they carried beneath them.

Liquid pain pumped through his heart.

"That's my baby!" Harrison's mother screeched as the bailiff and a guard held her arms. "You can't do that to *my* baby!"

"Order in this court!" The judge pounded and glared, but it had no effect. "Order, I said, or you'll be in contempt!"

"Nooo!"

Tears welled up in Harrison's eyes. He felt like a split stick of firewood, half shamed, half aching to hold her. He started toward his mother, but Mr. Constable's big hand clamped down on the back of his neck so that the nerves tingled in his head.

"Bailiff, remove that woman and take her into custody for contempt. I'll not have it in my courtroom. I'll *not* have it." The judge pounded a final time as they dragged her out. Then he cleared his throat, gave an accusing look to Mr. Constable, and asked the clerk for the next case.

Mr. Constable steered Harrison from the courtroom and all the way outside into the sunshine. A light breezed whispered through the trees, making the whole thing seem like a dream.

"Where's my mother?" Harrison asked.

"It's all right, Mud. You got a new mother now, Mrs. Constable. She's your mother by law."

It was too much. Having a complete and legal family should provide comfort and nourishment for his soul, but it didn't. Harrison thought of a snake he'd discovered under some boards behind the barn, a small snake that had swallowed a whole rat. It sat like a lump, helpless and unable to move for weeks, until it could finally digest its prey. He was that snake.

Harrison's new status seemed to include sitting up front in the truck. He leaned his head against the glass without feeling the bumps and bangs, even as they climbed the hole-filled driveway to the farm.

Mr. Constable slowed down by the barn. "Chores."

"What about school?" Harrison asked.

"You're excused for court."

"But we're done."

Mr. Constable reached across the seat and grabbed a handful of Harrison's trimmed hair at the back of his head, twisting it until his head thumped sideways against the dashboard. Mr. Constable moved his face close, also tilting it so they both looked at the world in the same knocked-over way. "You're done givin' me lip, you understand?"

Harrison nodded his head.

"Say it."

"I understand."

"I understand, sir."

"I understand . . . sir."

Mr. Constable turned him free. Harrison spilled from the truck, tripped, and fell to the ground.

"Chores." Mr. Constable reached across the seat and yanked the door shut. Harrison sat dusting himself off as the truck pulled away toward the house.

He didn't know all the reasons why Mr. Constable wanted to adopt him, but he knew without a doubt that it would somehow end in the Constables getting more money from some charity or government program. He knew all the kids on the farm had started out as foster kids, only to be adopted by the Constables for some unspoken reason. While they didn't seem to mind, Harrison had never—and would never—stop thinking of Melinda Johnson as his one and only true mother. He would no more think of himself as Harrison Constable than he would as Mud Johnson, let alone Mud Constable.

Cyrus's switch whistled through the air and snapped against the barn door. "I heard 'chores' mentioned. I'm busy with the vet. I need hay for the calves and I need it now."

Without speaking, Harrison got to his feet and headed for the hay barn. He loaded several bales onto a wheelbarrow and bounced it across the barnyard to where the veal calves sat tied to the little plastic capsules that kept them out of the rain. With a pitchfork, he broke down the bales and scattered hay at the feet of each calf.

Finished, he put the pitchfork over his shoulder and headed for the noise in the milk barn. When he arrived, he saw Cyrus and the vet down in the parlor working on a cow whose head had been clamped down between some bars. The cow was having a calf, but something had gone wrong and the men shouted and hurried back and forth. Mr. Constable stood at the railing above, looking down with a stem of grass in his teeth. He turned and scowled at Harrison.

"I said 'chores.'"

"I finished feeding the calves." Harrison couldn't

help but notice the cow's violent kick and the vet's quick movement to dodge it.

"No, you're lying again."

Harrison's face felt hot. "I'm not lying. I finished."

Mr. Constable pointed behind Harrison at the box stalls where they kept sick animals. "Them two sick calves ain't fed yet. Lying again. I said I won't have it, and I won't."

Mr. Constable started to loosen his belt.

"No." Harrison shook his head.

"No? I'll show you, no."

"*You* lied!" Harrison surprised himself as the shout rose above the braying cow and the excited men, who both looked up from the parlor. "You said for me to call you 'Papa.' That's a *lie!*"

Mr. Constable's belt whipped out at him—not the leather part, but the buckle itself, a treat only for the most special occasions. When it licked Harrison's forehead, blood spurted from his skin and one eye went dark.

Harrison wasn't exactly sure what happened after that. He knew he used the pitchfork, and he heard Mr. Constable scream in pain as two of the tines buried themselves in his leg. Why he flipped backward over the railing Harrison couldn't imagine, but he did. Harrison didn't blame himself for the cow. It was a wild cow, mad with pain from a bad birth, and Mr. Constable fell into it and the cow kicked him with all its might.

The crack of Mr. Constable's skull was what Harrison remembered most, like a cobblestone split by a heavy sledgehammer.

And then the blood . . . and the screams . . . and the words. In the madness, at one point Mrs. Constable grabbed his ears and pulled his face close to hers so she could spit her hot words directly in his face.

"You *killed* him!"